03

To Forget Is Annette

SPY CLASSROOM

code name
FORGETTER

code name
DREAMSPEAKER

SPY 03
CLASSROOM

To Forget Is Annette

Takemachi
ILLUSTRATION BY: **Tomari**

YEN
ON
New York

SPY CLASSROOM 03

Translation by Nathaniel Thrasher
Cover art by Tomari
Assistance with firearm research: Asaura

SPY KYOSHITSU Vol.3 <<BOGA>> NO ANETTO
©Takemachi, Tomari 2020
First published in Japan in 2020 by KADOKAWA CORPORATION, Tokyo.
English translation rights arranged with KADOKAWA CORPORATION, Tokyo through TUTTLE-MORI AGENCY, INC., Tokyo.

English translation © 2022 by Yen Press, LLC

Yen On
150 West 30th Street
New York, NY 10001

Visit us at yenpress.com
facebook.com/yenpress
twitter.com/yenpress
yenpress.tumblr.com
instagram.com/yenpress

First Yen On Edition: May 2022

Yen On is an imprint of Yen Press, LLC.
The Yen On name and logo are trademarks of Yen Press, LLC.

Library of Congress Cataloging-in-Publication Data
Names: Takemachi, author. | Tomari, Meron, illustrator. | Thrasher, Nathaniel Hiroshi, translator.
Title: Spy classroom / Takemachi ; illustrated by Tomari ; translation by Nathaniel Thrasher.
Other titles: Spy kyoushitsu. English
Description: First Yen On edition. | New York, NY : Yen On, 2021.
Identifiers: LCCN 2021021119 | ISBN 9781975322403 (v. 1 ; trade paperback) |
    ISBN 9781975322427 (v. 2 ; trade paperback) | ISBN 9781975338824
    (v. 3 ; trade paperback)
Subjects: | CYAC: Spies—Fiction. | Schools—Fiction.
Classification: LCC PZ7.1.T343 Sp 2021 | DDC [Fic]—dc23
LC record available at https://lccn.loc.gov/2021021119

ISBNs: 978-1-9753-3882-4 (paperback)
       978-1-9753-3883-1 (ebook)

10 9 8 7 6 5 4 3 2 1

LSC-C

Printed in the United States of America

C O N T E N T S

Prologue

Disappearance 1

Chapter 1

Appeal 5

Interlude

Missing ① 45

Chapter 2

Reunion 49

Interlude

Missing ② 55

Chapter 3

Mother and
Daughter 59

Interlude

Missing ③ 89

Chapter 4

Schism 97

Interlude

Missing ④ 139

Interlude

Villain 143

Chapter 5

A Battle Against
Great Evil 149

Epilogue

Forgetter 179

Next Mission 197

Afterword 203

SPY CLASSROOM
Specialized lessons for an impossible mission
Code name: Forgetter

Prologue

Disappearance

Their allies were gone.

As Klaus calmly accepted that fact, he took a seat on one of the sofas in Heat Haze Palace's main hall.

His expression was dour at the best of times, but at the moment, it was especially stern. He sat with his legs crossed, not so much as twitching. His eyes were closed, and one could have been fooled into thinking he was asleep if not for the fact that he intermittently opened his eyes, glanced over at the radio sitting on the table, then closed his eyes again. He took no other actions.

The sound of a violin performance streamed from the radio's speakers. Radio broadcasts had come into popularity during the Great War so that civilians could learn about the situation on the ground, and after the war ended, entertainment programs became a key tool for raising the people's flagging spirits while they recovered from the ravages of war. Such programs would normally inspire joy and good cheer, but at the moment, Klaus was deriving neither.

After what felt like hours, the performance ended, and the morning news broadcast finally began. However, all it contained were reports on the nation's economic climate with no useful information to be gleaned from them.

"If something happened, it wasn't big enough to make the news," Klaus concluded.

He was accompanied in the hall by a quartet of girls; they huddled around the table and stared restlessly at the radio.

The five of them were members of the spy team Lamplight.

Lamplight was a newly formed team that answered to the Din Republic's intelligence agency, the Foreign Intelligence Office. It was made up of Klaus and eight girls, and it specialized in taking on ultra-difficult Impossible Missions. Just two weeks ago, they had succeeded in capturing a foreign spy named Corpse and thwarting the assassination he was trying to commit.

While they were closing the book on that operation, however, four of the girls went missing.

They had been scheduled to return the night prior, but when morning rolled around, they were still nowhere to be seen, and they hadn't called ahead to say they would be late.

There was no other way to put it—they were missing.

"I mean, maybe they just forgot what day they were supposed to come back..."

The hopeful comment came from the silver-haired girl, Lily. Her most notable characteristics were her charming appearance and her sizable bosom.

Klaus shook his head. "That would be my first thought if *you* were the one AWOL, but you aren't."

"Wow, rude."

"The four we're missing would never make a blunder like that. Given who we're talking about, we should assume that they aren't calling because they aren't *able* to."

During the previous mission, Klaus had split the team in two.

There were the four members skilled enough to go up against Corpse—and the four members coordinated enough to get by without Klaus.

The missing group was the former one. It was hard to imagine those four forgetting to at least call.

The redheaded Grete summed up her thoughts as she brewed some black tea. "Then something...or some*one*...must be stopping them." Her limbs were long and slender, and she gave off the same sort of transient impression as a delicate piece of glasswork. "Please, Boss, is there anything more you can tell us? How did you all spend your last month together?"

The other girls nodded in agreement. The intimidating white-haired girl—Sybilla—shot Klaus a piercing stare, and the timid brown-haired girl—Sara—looked at him worriedly.

"That's right, I've been meaning to ask you!"

Lily leaned forward as she spoke.

"Why the heck is my room all blown up?"

"
...."

Klaus took his cup and sipped from it. "You know, Grete, this tea of yours is really quite delight—"

"Don't go changing the subject!" Lily cried.

"There was...a mishap."

"*Mishaps* don't blow up people's rooms!"

As Lily's angry bellow echoed in his ears, Klaus thought back.

The outer wall of Lily's room had been destroyed, leaving it completely exposed to the elements. Her bed was in splinters, her personal effects were scattered about the garden outside, and her scorched clothes lay in messy heaps.

When they got back to Heat Haze Palace the night prior, the sight had given Lily such a shock that her legs gave out under her.

Klaus began telling them everything—what had happened during the month Lily and the others were gone and, incidentally, why Lily's room was in pieces.

Chapter 1

Appeal

"Sara, I'll send your pets along later via courier."

Between her long, lustrous black hair, her body's generous curves, and the allure positively dripping from her lips and the corners of her eyes, "Dreamspeaker" Thea was attractive by just about any measure. Although she was only eighteen, you certainly wouldn't know it by looking at her.

When Grete, Sybilla, Sara, and Lily got picked for the Corpse mission and she didn't, Thea took the initiative and started backing them up however she could.

"I've also arranged for all your weapons to be delivered later under the name of a fictitious shipping company. Oh, and Sybilla, I'll add in a first aid kit in case your arm gets worse."

She got everything ready for them, diligently working to make sure they had everything they needed.

There was a common refrain heard around Heat Haze Palace: "Are we *sure* Thea isn't team leader?"

Klaus had introduced the "leader" position somewhat arbitrarily, and for whatever reason, he had appointed Lily to it. The team had a lot of questions, not least of which was *Why do we need a leader when we already have a boss?* but the ultimate consensus was that it was a meaningless title Klaus had simply made up as a way to motivate Lily.

None of the girls actually thought of Lily as their leader—aside from

Lily herself, who could often be heard muttering, "Heh-heh. 'Leader'…
What a beautiful ring that has."

In truth, though, Thea was the one who acted as the team's glue.

She had a naturally caring personality, but that wasn't all. There was
also her position as one of the two most attractive members of their
ranks, as well as the way that position helped accentuate both her
clear, resonant voice and her proactive approach to socializing with
the others. And what's more, she was also tied with Grete as the oldest
of the girls. All those factors worked together to make her the team's
leader in everything but name.

"Good hunting, everyone. Make sure you all come back here in one
piece, now, you hear?"

After working tirelessly to help them until the last possible moment,
she joined her comrades as they were about to leave.

She gave her fellow Intel Squad member, Grete, one final piece of
advice.

"Grete, don't push yourself out there. Make sure you coordinate well
with Teach."

"Of course. And thank you for seeing us off."

Then Thea spotted the pained look on Lily's face. "Hmm? Lily, what's
wrong? You look a little down."

"Oh, nah, it's nothing." Lily hurriedly waved her off, then quietly
continued. "I was worried, y'know? I thought this whole selection
thing might make things awkward between us all. So I was kinda surprised at how upbeat you sounded…"

"My, how unlike you. Why not just be your usual thoughtless self?"

"Phrasing!"

"Worry not, Lily. Teach picked you, and that's reason enough to
hold your head high. I promise, I'm not mad or anything. If nothing
else, I'm proud of you for having your hard work acknowledged."

Thea's encouragement seemed to do the trick in clearing up Lily's
worries.

Her expression brightened like a flower coming into bloom—

"You got it! Chosen Wunderkind Lily, over and out and ready to get
'er done!"

—and with that, she charged right out the entrance.

The other three waved good-bye to Thea, then hurried along
after her.

Thea watched them go, smiling a gentle smile designed to set their hearts at ease. And once they were gone—

"...They're gone, right?"

—she let out a quiet whisper. She opened the door a hair and made sure Lily and the others were completely out of sight.

After that, she headed to the main hall.

She stood beside one of its sofas and took a deep breath.

Then she went completely limp, collapsed onto the sofa—

"I'M SO MAAAAAAAAAD!"

—and screamed.

"It's too much! I can't take it! I don't know what to believe in anymore! I tried so hard for so long, and I didn't make the cut! I was so sure he'd pick me! I hate it! I hate it! I hate iiiiiit!"

She swung her arms and legs up and down, slamming them into the sofa again and again.

"Why wasn't I good enough, huh? I put in all the work, didn't I?"

Thea was throwing a childish tantrum.

She'd been holding it in ever since the announcement of who got selected, but now she had reached her breaking point.

All her composure had been an act. It had taken every bit of tooth gritting and fist clenching she had to resist the urge to scream.

The selection didn't make sense to her. Why hadn't she made the cut? How did Sybilla get the nod, considering her wound? Why had Lily, who couldn't walk two steps without tripping over herself, been chosen over her?

Thea had a lot of questions, but one thing was abundantly clear.

"Teach doesn't respect my skills one bit!"

And with that being the case—

"He only picked me for the team at all because he was after my body!"

—a possibility flashed through her mind.

She was onto something.

"It all makes sense now! So *that's* why Teach surrounded himself with eight girls who had nowhere else to go! You know, I always thought this living situation with one guy and a bunch of girls was like one of those smutty novels! It's obscene! Why, he's a sex-crazed fiend!

And to think, if he had come on a little gentler, I would have been like putty in his—"

"Enough of that."

Midway through her rant, Klaus appeared out of nowhere. The moment he did, the sofa tilted to the side.

Thea tumbled to the floor. Her eyes went wide.

"T-Teach...? How much of that did you catch?"

"Is that really a question you want to be asking after shouting loud enough for the entire manor to hear?" He gave her a look of utmost exasperation.

As waves of bashfulness and shame washed over her, he went on.

"Pull yourself together. I have an important job for you."

The world was awash in pain.

Ten years had passed since the end of the Great War, the largest war in human history. Seeing its horrors had driven the world's politicians to turn to spy work rather than military might as their preferred way of influencing other countries.

Nations the world over poured resources into their intelligence agencies, leading to an age of shadow wars fought between spies.

Lamplight was a spy team that fought on behalf of the Din Republic.

They specialized in Impossible Missions—missions that their fellow countrymen had failed to complete—and they had just been tasked with killing an assassin named Corpse. After careful consideration, Klaus selected four of the girls—Grete, Lily, Sybilla, and Sara—and sent them to work at a major politician's mansion.

However, he now revealed that that was merely a diversion.

"The truth is, you four are the ones who will actually be fighting Corpse."

Thea and the other three remaining girls sat in the main hall as they listened to his announcement.

Klaus explained the situation in full.

Corpse had an ally who helped him plan and carry out his assassinations, and Grete's team was going to go work for a big politician so they could root the ally out and expose them. By concealing the truth from Lily and the others, they would be able to trick Corpse's ally into thinking Klaus was there, too.

"I'm bringing the four of you with me to take on Corpse."

Thea breathed a sigh of relief. "Ah, so that's what this was all about. Now I finally understand."

As it turned out, she hadn't been forsaken after all. The incongruous pieces were finally clicking into place.

"It all makes sense now. That's a clever idea you came up with, Teach. I never doubted you for a moment."

"You sounded pretty doubtful just a moment ago."

"...Let's pretend that didn't happen."

"Corpse is a ruthless assassin. You need to make sure you keep your cool at all times." Klaus gave Thea a pointed look. "The most dangerous thing about Corpse is their complete willingness to kill civilians. If murdering dozens of unrelated people will let them bring down their target, they'll do it without a second thought. Our task this mission is nonnegotiable—capture Corpse without letting a single person die."

According to the dossier, Corpse had put down scores of the Empire's foes, spies, and politicians alike.

"Meeting that requirement will be difficult, make no mistake. That's why I've prepared a little test."

"What kind of test?"

"The kind where if you don't complete it by sundown, you won't be coming on the mission."

Thea gasped.

She could tell he was being serious. Klaus had already completed no small percent of the team's missions solo, and despite the risks involved, he would doubtless be willing to take on Corpse the same way.

Klaus held up his palm. "The test is simple. All you have to do is touch my hand."

Their normal itinerary was to make him say *I surrender*, and this task was even easier than that.

However, *easier* and *easy* were two vastly different things. This time around, they only had half a day to work with and only four members to do it with.

Thea started panicking. She didn't know if they were going to be up to—

"I have complete confidence that you'll be able to do it. Remember, I only chose the strongest."

"........."

Thea could hear the earnestness in his voice, and she felt a fire welling up inside her.

He's right... After all, I won. I mean, no offense to the four who didn't get picked, but my skills were recognized.

She clenched her fists tight.

After handling all their missions on his own for so long, Klaus was finally ready to rely on them, and if that wasn't enough of an honor already, she was one of the four chosen ones. Anyone would feel joy at receiving acknowledgment from someone as skilled as him.

She could do this.

She was going to pass his test, and she was going to take down Corpse.

"Just you wait. That was a pretty sorry display I put on just now, but that's all behind me. I won't let you down."

"Magnificent."

As she watched Klaus nod in satisfaction, Thea combed back her hair with her hand.

Her heart pounded, and she turned around to inspire her teammates.

"All right, everyone! Let's get this strategy meeting underway! With our skills, I'm sure we can—," Thea trailed off.

"...Huh?"

She cocked her head.

They were gone. Her three teammates, who'd just been sitting on the sofa, were nowhere to be seen.

"........................"

She was at a loss for words.

Had they seriously gone back to their rooms? When the discussion wasn't over? What were they planning on doing about the test?

"There's something you should know." Klaus's voice was matter-of-fact. "The four of you I picked are all extremely skilled. Aside from you, though, their teamwork leaves a lot to be desired."

"But..."

"Monika, Erna, and Annette all ran into problems in their academies due to how poorly they worked together with others."

And there she had it.

Now that he mentioned it, he was right. All the Lamplight members who excelled at cooperation were gone.

"If we're going to fight Corpse, your teamwork needs to be rock-solid."

"Oh, I absolutely agree, but you can't mean..."

Thea had a bad feeling about this. Klaus walked away almost evasively, and as he reached for the door, he gave her one final order.

"Bring the team together, Thea."

"...This is the 'important job' you were talking about?"

Realizing that her task was even harder than first advertised, Thea let out a deflated moan.

Thea cradled her head in her hands as she walked down the hallway.

...Now that I think about it, all the times I acted as a leader were when we had the whole team there.

She was well aware of the leadership role she held. As one of the oldest members of the group, she felt she had a responsibility to look out for her younger allies who hadn't totally outgrown childhood yet.

She definitely had qualms about the fact that Lily had been chosen as the team's official leader, but the leader in question had been so delighted by the designation that Thea had chosen to honor Klaus's choice by supporting the team in secret. She knew that was the mature thing to do. That girl nobody really respected could take the credit while Thea kept the team on the rails.

Thea didn't have any complaints about her role. At the moment, though, it left her in a bit of a pickle.

Lily and Sybilla aren't here to lighten the mood...

The two of them caused her a fair amount of worry, but the way they held the team's spirits up was undeniable. Lily's antics kept things upbeat, and that combined with Sybilla's lively snark had become something of a regular routine of theirs. When you added in Sara's adorable reactions, it was hard not to have a smile on your face.

Now that they were gone, Thea realized for the first time just how much of an asset that had been.

And to make matters worse, Grete was one of the only people capable of holding a decent conversation. With her absence, the team was basically in shambles.

Plus, the remaining members all have a few screws loose...

Thea squeezed her brow as she continued onward.

I suppose I should start with the easiest one to talk to and work my way up.

She headed to her first target's room, but for some reason, it was empty. It didn't look like she had gone out for a walk or anything, but she definitely wasn't there. After wandering around for a bit, Thea heard noise coming from—of all places—Lily's room.

She opened the door and found her target lying on Lily's bed.

"What, you need something?"

It was the cerulean-haired girl: Monika, code name Glint.

She had a medium build and no notable characteristics to speak of. Her entire appearance was designed to avoid giving off any hint of her personality. The one distinctive thing about her was her asymmetrical hairstyle, but even that was difficult to succinctly describe.

She looked completely average, and yet she didn't look like anything at all. It was like her very presence was aloof.

She inclined her head toward Thea without getting up.

"Do I *need* something?" Thea planted a hand on her hip. "Well, for starters, what are you doing in Lily's room?"

"Investigating."

"Investigating what?"

Monika was holding a pencil and scrawling on a notepad as she reclined.

"I figured I should go back over things, now that everyone's gone."

"Go over Heat Haze Palace, you mean?"

"It's nothing important, though. What do you want?"

Monika changed the subject, clearly not keen to reveal any more than that.

"I want to talk things over. I thought that would be obvious. We need to figure out how we're going to pass this test."

"C'mon, do we really need to talk that over?"

"Don't you *want* to pass the test?"

"Sure I do, but working together with you all isn't going to be enough to get me there."

"Well, don't just go deciding that on your own!"

That was it, right there.

That was Monika's personality flaw: her shameless arrogance.

She constantly looked down on her teammates, didn't have a humble bone in her body, and was as rude as all get out. She had the skills to back up her attitude, but that only pissed off the people around her more. Thea also had complicated feelings about the fact that, at sixteen, Monika was two years her junior.

"You can brag all you want; you'll just make a fool of yourself." Thea raised her voice. "If you're here in Lamplight, it means you washed out of your academy like the rest of us."

"I told you, remember? I was pulling my punches, that's all."

"Oh? And what about the little birdie who told me you couldn't play well with others?"

"That's not it. They just couldn't keep up with me."

"Heh. That sounds like an excuse, is what that sounds like."

"………"

Monika went silent.

Did the jab land? Thea had been intentionally trying to get under Monika's skin, but Monika's expression was as level as ever.

Monika held out her hand.

"Gimme a coin," she said. "I'll flip; you call."

"And if I call it right, you'll help us?"

"If you call it wrong, you leave me alone."

Thea tossed her a coin, and Monika flipped it without so much as sitting up. A satisfying *cling* rang out as the coin spun up into the air.

When it reached its apex—

"Heads."

—Thea called it.

The coin descended...only to land upright in a crack in the floor.

"——!"

"Can you leave now? I'm gonna work alone."

Monika waved Thea off in annoyance. By the look of it, she had pulled that unbelievable stunt intentionally. She didn't even seem surprised at the result.

She returned to her notepad, having lost all interest in Thea.

Talking things over with Monika had ended in failure, so Thea turned to door number two.

Unlike Monika, the problem with Thea's second target didn't lie with their own personality. In her case, the issue was with her interpersonal *skills*.

When Thea returned to the main hall, she found the girl she was looking for lurking behind the sofa with the top of her head peeking up from its back. It was a rather surreal sight, seeing a sofa with a partial head of blond hair.

"Erna, do you mind if we chat for a minute?"

Thea spoke softly so as not to scare Erna as she approached her.

All of a sudden, the blond hair whooshed as Erna scampered over behind a different sofa. She reminded Thea of a rabbit hiding in a patch of brush.

"Errrnaaaa! ♪" She tried again.

However, the blond head of hair skillfully fled once more. Her reflexes were impressive. By the time Thea finishing taking a single step, Erna was already gone and hiding behind a new sofa. Thea tried and tried, but she could never get so much as a decent glimpse of her quarry's face.

She continued undeterred, and eventually—

"Ow!"

—the blond yelped.

One of her shoes had slipped clean off. It tumbled through the air, its shoelace torn in two in a stunning display of misfortune. Thea's target collapsed facedown onto the carpet.

After soaring through the air, the shoe ultimately landed directly atop the target's head. She let out a dejected murmur. "How unlucky..."

It was the blond-haired girl: Erna, code name Fool.

At long last, Thea was able to get a good look at her. Her childish looks belied her fourteen years of age, and her bright-blond hair and near-translucent skin made one think of a beautiful little doll.

She was also exceedingly shy.

After redonning her shoe, she hid back behind the sofa.

"You know, if you keep running away like that, you're going to hurt my feelings."

"...I'm sorry." The voice rose up from the other side of the sofa. "But I'm calmer when I don't have to look people in the eye."

"I see. Don't you normally talk just fine, though?"

"Urk... That's the last thing an antisocial person likes to hear..."

"Antisocial? How do you mean?"

"There are all sorts of different types, but…in my case, I get talkative with people I'm close to, and I can talk in group settings just fine, and if I work up my courage, I can greet people I pass on the street."

"That sounds plenty social to me…"

"But! The scariest thing is talking one-on-one with teammates I'm not that close with yet!"

"Ah, so it's complicated."

"Plus, being told that I normally talk just fine is the most embarrassing thing of all!"

The visible bit of Erna's head quivered.

Apparently, antisocial people each had their own particular quirks.

Erna's predisposition for unluckiness—which was actually a predisposition for self-flagellation, apparently?—had caused her to grow up without developing proper social skills. In a sense, it wasn't really her fault.

"The only people I can really talk to are Teach and Big Sis Sara."

Upon hearing Erna's explanation, Thea shook her head. Sara wasn't there. She was going to have to lead the conversation herself.

"What if we started with something simple, then?"

"I-I'll do my best."

At long last, Thea managed to get a concession out of her teammate.

However, that much made sense. Erna's interpersonal skills might have been lacking, but she was fundamentally a friendly person.

"For example… What do you and Teach usually talk about?"

"Nothing special." The words came sparingly—and only a few at a time. "Mostly just the weather."

"Well, that's nice. It takes two people with good chemistry to be able to have a good conversation about the weather."

Either that or two people who were both terrible at conversations.

Thea suspected the latter was true here, but she chose not to voice that opinion aloud.

"Do you think you like Teach?"

"…I don't really get love. I tried asking Big Sis Sara about it, but that didn't help much."

"Oh, so that's the kind of stuff you and Sara talk about?"

"Big Sis Sara is really nice. She always sticks by my side."

It was clear from Erna's voice just how much she trusted their brown-haired teammate.

Lamplight was home to all sorts of loud personalities, so it made sense that she would find it comforting to be around someone like Sara.

Thea had a better understanding of the team's interpersonal relationships now. Over in the Specialist squad, Sara probably took on a sort of mediator role, and from what Thea had heard, she had a decent handle on one of the team's *other* difficult girl, as well.

Thea had saved the hardest for last, and if she wanted to win *her* over, she would need to start by getting Erna on her side.

The two or three pieces of small talk they'd gotten through should have lowered Erna's guard. It was time to get to the heart of the matter.

"By the way, Erna, about that test we're supposed to do—"

"Wow. I was actually able to talk for five whole minutes..."

As it turned out, it was actually Thea whose guard was down.

Erna looked at the ceiling with a vacant expression. Her voice was thick with fatigue.

"I'm tired now, so I'm going to take a nap."

"After just five minutes?"

Thea did her utmost to talk Erna out of this plan, but Erna was having none of it.

With keen, nimble movements, she fled the main hall.

Thea's legs felt like lead.

Two strikeouts in a row.

She had known it wasn't going to be easy, but she never imagined it would be *this* difficult. Those were the two more stable members she had to work with, and she hadn't even gotten through to them.

Rock-solid? We aren't rock anything...

At the moment, Corpse was the least of their concerns. They were falling apart before they'd even gotten to the starting line.

And worse, this last girl is the one who worries me most of all.

She was, without a doubt, the biggest problem child on Lamplight.

Although their entire team was composed of academy washouts, this last girl managed to stand out even among *their* ranks.

No, no. I mustn't give up before I even try talking to her. We're teammates, aren't we? I'm sure I can get through to her!

Thea tried to encourage herself so she could push past her back-to-back losses.

I can do it. I know I can! Teach wouldn't have picked me if I wasn't up to the job!

She gave her cheeks a clap and headed for the last girl's bedroom.

The room was tucked away in a back corner of Heat Haze Palace. Its occupant had originally picked a room closer to the manor's center, but a series of noise complaints had led to her forceful relocation. The room's resident cared little about privacy, and she always left her door wide open. Sleeping, changing, it didn't matter to her.

Thea knocked on the wall, then stepped in.

Her target was sleeping in the middle of the room…suspended from the ceiling.

"……………"

The acrid smell of oil assaulted Thea's nose.

The room was by no means small, and it was stacked high with miscellaneous gadgetry. Most of it looked like junk, but looks could be deceiving. Either way, though, the engines, gears, copper wire, and springs were all pieced together and piled into veritable mountains. If Thea strained her eyes, she could just barely make out what looked like a bed peeking out from beneath the miscellanea.

It would seem there was so much scrap lying around that the room's bed had become unusable, leading its resident to set up a hammock to use instead. However, half her body had fallen out of it, leaving her in the current state of suspension.

"Come on, Annette, rise and shine. If you nap too much, you won't be able to sleep well at night."

Thea jostled the girl's shoulders, fighting against the urge to just give up and leave.

The hanging girl's eyes snapped open, and she wriggled her legs free from the hammock they were tangled up in. It looked as though she was going to fall, but she twisted her body at the last moment and landed gracefully atop the floor.

"I'm up, yo!"

It was the ash-pink-haired girl: Annette.

Annette's appearance was so conspicuous it was hard to believe she was actually a spy. She was long overdue for a haircut, and her hair hung in a pair of pigtails that curled as though through force of will. Due to some sort of old injury or something, she could never be found without her eye patch. It would be hard to find a single spy anywhere more immediately identifiable than her.

She was super adorable...as long as she didn't open her mouth.

"Say, Annette, can we—?"

"Oh, hey, Sis." Annette cut her off and gave her an angelic smile. "That thing you're standing on is a bomb I made, yo."

"You have *what* just lying around?!"

"Well, from your right, there's Stun Gun Knife Mk. 4, the Fountain Pen Mega Blowtorch, a bazooka that can destroy anything, Super Parachute Mk. 3—"

"I wasn't asking for an inventory!"

Thea hurriedly distanced herself from the gadgets strewn across the floor. Apparently, all of them were Annette's inventions.

It felt like walking through a minefield, but she eventually reached a spot where the floor was visible.

"By the way, Annette, can I ask why you went back to your room just now?"

Annette picked up the empty milk bottle lying on the ground and lifted it up high. "I wanted some warm milk."

"I see..." Thea couldn't work up the will to get mad at her. She didn't know where to start. "Next time you wander off, I want you to make sure you tell me first."

"You got it!"

"This mission isn't going to be easy. Are you sure you're ready for it?"

"You got it!"

"...You aren't just blowing me off, are you?"

"Nope!"

"Jump."

"You got it!" Annette hopped into the air.

"Spin."

"You got it!" Annette twirled to the side.

"Strip."

"You got it!" Annette started to take off her clothes, but Thea put a quick stop to that.

She was at a loss.

"How does this girl's brain even work?"

That was one of Annette's other notable characteristics—she was *innocent to a fault, free-spirited as could be,* and *utterly inscrutable.*

She would take things at face value that she really should have questioned. She would go on dangerous missions without so much as faltering. She would accept bizarre orders and carry them out without hesitating. But then, just when you thought you had her figured out, she would refuse requests for no reason at all and go off and do her own thing. She also had curiosity in spades and could often be found building inventions that defied all rhyme and reason.

According to Klaus, Annette didn't remember anything from before she enrolled in her spy academy. Her code name was Forgetter, and she certainly lived up to it. Her papers listed her as being fourteen, but her actual age was a mystery as she'd been taken in by the state with no memories or birth certificate.

Not only was she herself inscrutable, her background was, too. Such was the nature of this girl Annette.

I need to figure out some way to start a dialogue with her...

As Thea brooded over what to do, Annette tilted her head and gave her a quizzical look.

"Not feelin' good, Sis?"

"I suppose I've felt better, yes."

Without even a hint of reservation, Annette slapped Thea's cheek, then backhanded it for good measure. Afterward, she gave her diagnosis. "According to me, you don't have a cold."

Her speech patterns, appearance, and actions all defied explanation.

However, she had just expressed concern about Thea's well-being. She clearly at least cared about her teammates. Thea chose to bet on that one ray of hope.

"You know, Annette, I'm having some trouble with Teach's test. Could you help me out?"

"I tried that already, yo."

"You did?"

Now, that was a surprise.

Thea had assumed she'd forgotten all about the test. Perhaps she was taking this more seriously than Thea had given her credit for.

"What did you do? How did you approach it?"

"I asked Klaus, 'Bro, can I touch your hand?'"

"Uh…"

"He said no, though."

Of course he did. Wouldn't be much of a test otherwise.

"I'm so mad, I'm going to bed!"

With that, Annette hopped back into the hammock. Once again, half her body slipped out and left her dangling in the air, but she went to sleep like it was the most comfortable thing in the world.

"……………"

The sound of Thea's heart snapping in two echoed through the room.

"I can't do it… There's no way I can corral those three… It can't be done…"

Thea squatted in front of the cage full of mice.

She had believed that her leadership skills would allow her to bring her uncooperative teammates together, but that dream lay dashed. Now she realized just how much her past achievements had hinged on the efforts of her currently absent allies. On her own, she could barely even get her teammates to talk to her.

It hurt. She wanted to cry. She wanted someone to swoop in and save her.

"…I'm doing my best, but they just won't help me…"

"Well, don't come crying to me about it."

The blunt response she got came from the person beside her who was gently carrying the mice—Klaus.

The two of them were at the animal pen just outside of Heat Haze Palace proper.

It had originally been used as a storehouse, but Sara—the girl who specialized in dealing with animals—had remodeled it so she could keep her pets there. There would normally have been a dog and a hawk there, too, but they were off on a mission with Sara, so the pen was currently empty save for a quintet of mice.

"I have to get these mice to the handler by this afternoon. I'm sorry, but I don't have time for this right now."

There was a hint of annoyance in Klaus's voice.

They would be leaving Heat Haze Palace tomorrow, so there would be nobody there to look after Sara's animals. They would need someone to watch them until Lamplight got back—presuming that Thea and the others could pass Klaus's test, of course.

In order to get ready for that, the team's boss was making the necessary preparations himself. He didn't so much as turn to look at Thea.

"Between this and that unsightly display earlier, you really need to work on your mental fortitude."

"You think I don't know that?"

This wasn't the first time a minor setback had sent Thea into a tailspin. Throughout the team's training with Klaus, she often ended up sulking after their losses.

"Say, Teach…" Thea's voice took on a sultry tone. "…Don't you think you could gently console me?"

"No." Klaus shot her down in heartbeat.

She glared at him resentfully. "This is the first time a man's ever been so cruel to me when I was down."

"And what did all the other men do?"

"Oh, they were just lovely. They would compliment me aaaaall night long."

"Maybe that coddling is what made you so fragile." Klaus's blunt comment earned him another angry glare.

Thea knew she was attractive. Men always turned to stare when she was out and about, and with a tiny bit of work, she could start a relationship with over 90 percent of them. Lamplight had plenty of attractive young women in its ranks, and she prided herself on the fact that she was an easy top-two-er when it came to looks.

However, Klaus was like a brick wall.

Thea had tried to seduce him time and time again, but she had yet to get so much as a rise out of him.

"Have you considered exercising some self-control? As I recall, this is why your grades plummeted back at your academy."

"Look, that was hardly my fault. How was I supposed to know that the teacher I was going out with was married?"

"From what I hear, things got kind of ugly."

"You can say that again. I definitely learned my lesson there."

That was what had earned Thea the label of washout.

Whenever she went into town, she used it as an opportunity to sleep with men, and sometimes, those men happened to include her academy's male faculty. The way she saw it, it was all part of her training as a female spy, but one of her other teachers got mad at her impropriety and unjustly tanked her grades.

"In any case, I'm not taking you along if you can't pass the test. This mission will prove lethal if your teamwork isn't up to par." Klaus's voice was firm. "If worse comes to worst, I'll have to do it on my own."

"......"

"However, doing that will make it more dangerous. It'll mean Corpse will have more opportunities to kill innocent bystanders."

Thea let out a small moan at being reminded of the gravity of her task.

If they failed this test, people would die. That was the responsibility they bore as spies.

It was hard to imagine the superhuman Klaus actually *losing* to Corpse, but Corpse was all too willing to kill bystanders in order to mask their targets or make their getaway. Preventing that was going to take manpower.

"............"

Thea reached for Klaus's hand as he continued working.

He effortlessly slipped away.

She tried the brute-force approach a couple more times, but she was no match for his speed. She even knocked over a bucket of water and let out a suggestive cry, but Klaus ignored her. He had no interest in the way her wet skirt clung to her skin and natural curves.

Sure enough, she wasn't going to be able to do this alone.

She needed her teammates' help.

The problem was: How was she going to get it? How could she get them to work together when she couldn't even get any of them to hold a conversation?

"Thea." As she gnawed on her lip in frustration, Klaus called over to her. "I've been meaning to ask you something. As I recall, you knew a surprising amount about Inferno. Why is that?"

That was a rather abrupt change of subject.

"Hmm? Oh, yes." Thea nodded. "The thing is, I actually met them once."

She had told him several times about how much she admired Inferno.

"Seven years ago, Inferno saved my life. Do you not remember that incident where Imperial spies kidnapped the only daughter of a major newspaper's president, Teach?"

"...I'm not sure. I might have been on a different mission at the time."

"I don't remember you being there, so that might have been it. It was a woman with crimson hair who told me about Inferno."

A smile spread across Thea's face.

"I couldn't sleep, so she told me stories. She was the nicest person I ever met. She isn't just my savior; she's my idol."

Klaus glanced at her in surprise. "A woman with crimson hair? Using classified state secrets as bedtime stories? She's an unconventional one, that's for sure."

"I suppose it is odd, isn't it? Does that description ring any bells for you?"

"It does. That was code name Hearth, Inferno's boss."

Thea let out a little yelp of shock.

The woman had been fairly young, so Thea assumed she was just a lowly grunt. She never would have taken her for the boss of such a legendary spy team.

Klaus's eyes softened as nostalgia colored his expression.

"Thea, do you think Inferno's members always got along?"

"I never really thought about it..."

"We were as close as family, but there were still times we got under each other's skin or didn't see eye to eye. In fact, we fought all the time. The boss was a kind person by nature, but in arguments, she was as stubborn as a bull. We all had different opinions on things, so getting us on the same page was no easy feat, and we constantly butted heads."

"I have to say, that's pretty different from how I pictured it..."

"However, I don't think that was a bad thing at all," Klaus noted. *"Enjoy that discord. Differences between allies are the key to a strong team."*

The advice left a keen impression on Thea.

Klaus went on. "I cribbed that quote off the boss. The best approach is to butt heads with your teammates directly."

Now that she knew those words were Hearth's, she could feel them strike her right in the heart.

Immediately after leaving the animal pen, Thea spotted Monika.

In her hand, she was holding a wrench. Thea wanted to call out to her, but Monika headed back into the manor before she got a chance.

I wonder what she's been doing all this time?

Monika had said she was going to work alone, but it still annoyed Thea how she hadn't revealed anything more than that.

Thea brooded for a moment, then decided to head for Lily's room. That was where Monika had been earlier when she talked about "investigating." Thea wanted to see if she could figure out what Monika had been looking into.

In contrast with its owner's personality, Lily's room was spick-and-span, and the chemical vials on her shelf were lined up in neat rows. It was clear that, as a poisoner, she had the proper level of respect for how dangerous her tools were. She might not have looked it, but she was diligent where it counted.

The only thing out of order was the single scrap of paper lying on the ground. It was hard to imagine it being Lily's.

Is that from Monika's notepad...?

The first thing she found when she picked up and unfurled it was a list.

Taps: garden, kitchen, private bathroom, communal bath [X], bathroom

It was information about Heat Haze Palace.

It was unclear why Monika was choosing to investigate that after they'd been there for so long, and the X mark next to "communal bath" was a mystery as well. There wasn't one next to Klaus's private bathroom—just the girls' larger one.

As Thea skimmed the memo for other information of note, she found something that was even more of a surprise.

Lily: larger than other bedrooms. Old boss's room?

Thea looked up with a start.

Monika was investigating Inferno?

Just as the note said, Thea got the sense that Lily's room was a bit larger than all the others. That was due to its corner position on the second floor, no doubt. The room's upholstery was also all ornate, and it was clear at a glance just how high quality the bed was.

It was the kind of room that belonged to the person at the top of the residents' pecking order.

"Lily's bedroom was Ms. Hearth's bedroom?"

The room got a lot more sunlight than Klaus's, too.

As thoughts of how Lily shrewdly seized the manor's best room for herself and how Klaus still solitarily refused to change rooms himself swirled through Thea's mind, she surveyed the room in a daze.

My idol lived here... The person who made me want to become a spy...

That woman had saved her from the depths of hell itself.

She had been as warm as the sun, she had soothed Thea's terrified heart, and on top of that, she had been as fierce as hellfire herself. Thea couldn't help but be taken with her.

She still remembered the promise that woman had made her.

"If you hone that special talent of yours, you'll be the strongest spy around."

"But the thing is: I don't want you to become just any old spy."

"I want you to become a hero."

"If you can do that, then I'm sure we'll meet again. And when we do, I'll prepare a wonderful present for you."

That reunion never ended up happening, but Hearth's words still lived on in Thea's heart.

She had followed Hearth's instructions and continued training her special ability. All those past relationships hadn't been for pleasure. She had done it to polish her skills. And no matter how many times her spirit had gotten crushed, she had never stopped striving toward that ideal.

She was going to become a hero.

A hero, just like that crimson-haired spy who saved her.

"Ms. Hearth, you butted heads with your teammates, too, but that didn't stop you, did it?"

Thea's head was back in the game.

She stood in her idol's room and swore an oath. Right now, what she needed was the sheer self-assertiveness to make success an inevitability.

"You protected this nation's people before, and now it's my turn to hold the line. And I'm going to use the skill you helped me discover to do it."

An elegant smile spread across Thea's face as she made her proclamation.

"I'm code name Dreamspeaker—and it's time to lure them to their ruin."

Erna stood in the kitchen cooking lunch. There was no sense trying to pass a test on an empty stomach.

Even with half the girls gone, they still took turns preparing meals. It was important that they cook their food themselves. From what Erna heard, Lily and the others were currently working as maids. Being able to cook was an important part of a spy's arsenal.

"...................."

However, she was having trouble focusing. Her head was somewhere else entirely.

That was one of Erna's habits—holding mental postmortems.

I ended up running away from Big Sis Thea...

Erna was truly down about that. She shouldn't have been so rude.

I should have stayed and kept talking, shouldn't I have...?

She should have kept up her end of the conversation better. She should have given Thea a cute smile. Regrets washed over her one after another.

Even Klaus had told her she needed to get better at working with her teammates.

Back when they beat Guido, Erna had successfully pulled off a tag team with Lily. However, a large part of their synergy was simply due to Lily's complete disregard for other people's boundaries. Erna had barely had to do anything.

It would be awesome if she could work together with the others like that again, but—

Yeah, "but."

Before she could work up her resolve, she lost heart again.

If I get them caught up in my misfortune, they'll just abandon—

Right as that old niggling doubt started working its way through her mind like a curse, she heard a voice from behind her.

"Oh, if it isn't Erna."

"Yeeep!" Erna hadn't even noticed anyone coming.

Thea chuckled. "There's no need to look so startled. Are you on cooking duty today? Where's your partner?"

"It was supposed to be Big Sis Monika. She left a note that said *BRB* and disappeared."

"What, she blew you off?" Thea puffed out her cheeks in annoyance.

She was clearly trying to come across as joking and friendly, but it ended up having the opposite effect. Having her personal space invaded by someone she wasn't that close with sent Erna's heart pounding.

The kitchen was small. She had nowhere to run.

When Erna realized she was subconsciously trying to figure out an escape route, she shook her head.

N-no, I can't. I have to be brave...

She opened her mouth to try to get the words—any words—out, but Thea beat her to the punch with a quiet laugh.

"Erna, do you want to become close with me?"

Her voice had a very grown-up ring to it. Erna felt as though the words were coiling their way across her skin.

"Be honest. Would you want to be close with me, *even if it meant baring your innermost secrets?*"

"I..." Erna hesitated for a moment. "...I do. I want to."

"Okay. Then, can you be strong for three seconds?"

"Huh?"

"Can you look me in the eye for that long?"

Thea reached for Erna as she spoke. Erna instinctively started to flee, but she was able to fight off the urge.

Thea covered Erna's cheeks with her hands, practically swaddling them. Her fingers were cool on Erna's skin.

They looked like a couple about to kiss as Thea tilted Erna's face up and gazed at her, her eyes as clear as polished obsidian.

"Just like that." Thea's sweet whisper seeped into Erna's brain, which was on fire with embarrassment.

It was only going to be three seconds long.

To Erna, though, it felt like several minutes.

Had all the world's lovers gone through the same thing, Erna wondered? Her heart was beating out of her chest. It was like Thea's eyes were seeing right through her.

A slight chill ran across her skin.

It felt like Thea was peering directly into her heart.

"Erna." Thea's beguiling lips moved. "You really are adorable."

The three seconds were up, and Thea released Erna from her grasp.

Erna took a deep breath. She had tensed up so much she'd forgotten to breathe.

What was that all about, she wondered? As she stood there in a daze, Thea said something she could never have expected.

"You want a big sister, don't you?"

"Wha—?"

"That's why you call us all Big Sis, isn't it? What a needy girl you are. And you realize it, too. You realize that most fourteen-year-olds have grown up a whole lot more than you have. That must be hard on you. Wanting more and more to have someone dote on you, but having to make sure you control yourself and never let that feeling show..."

Thea laid it all out, not sparing any detail.

There was a fair amount of teasing and ridicule in her voice that lanced right into Erna's heart.

Erna's chest tightened.

Everything Thea just said was completely and totally true.

"That's..." As her anxiety rose, Erna spoke up. "That's not it... I just don't want to drag people into my misfortune..."

"Sure, and that's why your wish never came true. No matter hooow long you waited." Thea laughed mockingly. "What a child you are."

Erna's face went red.

An emotion welled up inside her so violently she couldn't even tell if it was shame or rage.

Why does she have to say those things?

Erna had lost her family at a young age. A fire broke out and claimed the lives of her parents, her elder sister, and her elder brother, leaving her the sole survivor. While other kids were growing up playing with their moms and their dads, Erna grew up alone.

Deep down, she wanted to be doted on, but she had spent her life suppressing that desire.

She thought it wasn't fair that she, and only she, managed to survive, and she'd been a prisoner to that belief for years.

Her brother and sister would never get a chance to smile again. It wouldn't be fair if only she got to be happy.

That was what had caused her to subconsciously seek punishment and why she was so drawn to accidents. The reason she had thrown herself headfirst into the harsh world of spycraft was because of her jumbled-up feelings of self-hatred and desire for atonement.

Why does she have to laugh at my pain?!

"That's not true. I—!"

"It's okay. I'll be your big sister."

Thea cut off Erna's angry shout by forcefully wrapping her in a hug.

Erna found herself pressed against Thea's plump bosom. A gentle, nostalgic aroma invaded her nostrils.

"None of the others have to know about this, and if you want to cry, they don't have to know about that, either. Anything for my adorable little sister."

"I…"

"There's no need to be shy. Just be honest with yourself. It's okay to let go."

Thea whispered right in her ear. Her lips were so close they were almost touching her, and her voice felt like it was resonating directly in Erna's brain.

"I can grant all the secret wishes you can't bring yourself to share."

The violent emotion that had welled up in Erna started fading.

Thea gently stroked Erna's back. Her fingers were gentle and comfortable. In all her life, nobody had ever touched Erna like that before.

Chills ran down Erna's spine. She wondered if they were from fear. It felt like her whole self was going to get overwritten.

However, she couldn't bring herself to fight it.

The faintly mocking sound of Thea calling her "little sister" still lingered in Erna's ears. The sweet, addictive tenor wormed its way into the cracks of her wounded heart.

That was as far as her thoughts went before she gradually stopped thinking altogether. The feeling of Thea's soft chest was like being curled up in a warm blanket. Erna's mind went blank.

The strength faded from her body, and she surrendered herself to her teammate.

Erna went limp in Thea's arms, her eyes vaguely empty.

Thea glanced down, then breathed a sigh of relief.

It worked.

She rarely used her ability on women or people younger than her, much less her own allies, but it looked like it had done the trick. That much was clear from the warmth she felt from Erna's body. All her worries about Thea had melted away.

After waiting a suitable amount of time, Thea let go of Erna. Erna seemed reluctant to leave her embrace, but after Thea gave her head a few pats, her face went red, and she got back to preparing lunch.

When Thea left the kitchen, she found Monika leaning against the hallway wall with an indignant look on her face.

"What'd you do to Erna?"

She must have seen all that. It made sense; after all, she *was* supposed to be on cooking duty.

Thea shook her head briefly.

"Just a little trick of mine, that's all. Nothing worth writing home about."

Thea had a special ability—the ability to see people's desires.

She could tell what they lusted for. What they coveted.

She wasn't able to get exact details, but she could generally get the broad strokes and figure out anything from a person's twisted fetishes to their secret aspirations. When she took that information and offered her target something corresponding with their desires, such as money or her body, she could have most people in the palm of her hand.

In short, she specialized in negotiations.

That was the skill Hearth had recognized in her.

"Would you like me to teach it to you? I know the perfect technique for winning men over, and I'd be more than happy to share it."

"That's gonna be a no from me."

"Oh, no, it's really all right. I'll have you know that I taught Grete everything she knows about seduction!"

"So you're the mastermind behind those pathetic displays of sexual harassment?"

"Don't call it pathetic! She's trying her best!"

Monika gave her a derisive sneer. "I don't need to learn your trick. It looks like a pain to use, and if it was actually that good at winning people over, you'd have beaten Klaus with it ages ago."

"It's depressing how quick on the uptake you are…"

Sure enough, Monika was right. Thea's technique had a condition attached.

To use it, she had to lock eyes with her target for three seconds.

Against men with ulterior motives for her, that requirement was more or less trivial. However, Klaus was so wary she hadn't been able to pull it off on him a single time, and in any sort of combat situation, it was as good as useless.

Once she cleared that hurdle, though, the skill was all but unbeatable.

Even Monika, for all her arrogant posturing, would be helpless before it.

Monika let out a small laugh. "What's with that look?" She had sensed that something was up, and a belligerent expression spread across her face. "You gonna try it on me? Go for it. See if you can tame me."

"I won't; don't worry. I wouldn't use it on a teammate without their permission."

That was a rule Thea had set for herself.

No good could come of rudely peering into her friends' hearts.

"Monika, if you're not going to help us, then fine. We'll work alone, too. Just make sure you don't get in our way."

"Well, that's boring." Monika stretched her arms up toward the ceiling. The gesture positively dripped with scorn. "If you're that pissed at me, you should've just made me submit by force."

"What are you talking about…?"

Thea assumed she was either joking or baiting her.

However, Monika's eyes told a different story. They were full of a contemptuous pity, as if Thea had her bored out of her mind.

"…This team's got nothing but good little girls on it, doesn't it?"

"What?"

"And you're probably the worst one. A prissy little lady playing her depraved little games of house. It makes me sick." Monika exhaled. "But it's not just you—it's everyone. Spies need to be ruthless, and that's something this team is sorely lacking. Makes a girl worry. You think we're going to stand a chance next time we run up against someone who doesn't play fair?"

After that harsh diatribe, she vanished down the hallway.

As she left, Thea spotted the wrench she was holding. Was she doing some sort of construction?

After Monika disappeared from view, her scornful voice echoed out behind her.

"If you're going to keep playing the good little girl, at least make yourself useful and look after the kids."

"If she has something she wants to say, why doesn't she just come out and say it?"

Monika had just piled some rather harsh abuse on Thea, and what's more, Thea wasn't entirely sure why.

Feelings of gloom rose up in her heart, but she didn't have time to deal with Monika right now. That was just who Monika was. Rather than trying to force her to play nice, it would be better to just leave her to her own devices.

There was something else Thea needed to prioritize right now.

There was someone she absolutely wanted to win over.

Each of the Lamplight girls had special skills that nobody else could hope to match.

Originally, the idea was to use them as a secret weapon against Guido. That man knew every other spy in the nation, but a group of washouts like them had a chance to take him by surprise.

Lily had her poison, Grete had her disguises, Sybilla had her theft, Thea had her negotiations...

Because their abilities were built off a combination of their innate talents and their specific backgrounds and origins, they were impossible to imitate. These skills were theirs and theirs alone.

However, three members of their ranks had such powerful skills that they put all the others to shame.

None of those three could hold their own in a fight, and none of them was particularly clever or resourceful. Furthermore, they were barely more than children emotionally, so they couldn't be left to operate independently. However, their devastating abilities alone were enough to provide their teammates with valuable backup.

Klaus had grouped the three of them into a team designed to provide logistical support from the rearguard: the Specialist squad.

There was Sara's rearing, Erna's accidents, and Annette's, well…

In Thea's opinion, Annette's talent was the most unfair one of the bunch.

Annette wasn't in her room. Instead, she was in the washroom. At first, it looked like she was washing her hands, but she was actually stooped down in front of the sink and dual-wielding screwdrivers.

When Thea got close, Annette violently swiveled her head to look at her.

"Oh, hey, it's Thea. What's up, Sis?"

"What are you doing down there?"

"The faucet was broken, so I'm fixing it, yo."

There was a vast array of parts and components scattered around Annette's feet. There were far more tools than she could have possibly needed for such a simple repair job.

However, what was even more concerning was—

"Is that three faucets there?"

Thea must have used that single faucet a hundred times, but now there were three of them.

They sat in a perfect row and all hung at the same angle. Thea couldn't even begin to tell which one was the original.

Annette explained. "They all look exactly the same, down to their shapes and scuff marks. But only one of them is right, and if you turn the wrong one, it explodes."

"You really are a genius, aren't you?" Thea sighed in amazement.

That was Annette's talent: tinkering.

Her bottomless curiosity had led her to become a master of meddling with machines. She could do everything from producing new spy gadgets to constructing new water and electric lines and painting them into perfect camouflage.

And that wasn't all.

As it turned out, her inventions were better than the most cutting-edge stuff Din was able to come up with.

It was hard to imagine her having developed her skills anywhere but abroad or with some sort of secret organization.

Annette didn't remember so much as where she was born, and those technical skills were the sole thing she'd retained. That was why she'd been recruited to the spy academies.

If she could use those skills in her spy work, who knows what she could accomplish…!

The idea was downright tantalizing.

The thing was, all she used her ability for were pranks and bizarre contraptions. She occasionally turned out some sort of ultra-high-quality device, but only on the rare occasion when the mood struck her.

It's up to me to guide her.

Thea renewed her resolve and spoke.

"Hey, Annette?"

"Yes?"

"Do you want to get close with me? Even if it means revealing a little of what's in your heart?"

"……………………………………………………"

Annette froze with the smile still plastered on her face. She didn't so much as twitch. It was like she was a machine that had just shut down. Her eyes were so glassy it was impossible to tell if they were even in focus.

"Yeah. I want to get close with you." After a long silence, Annette gave the go-ahead.

Thea exhaled. That was the first hurdle down. "All right, then, can you look me in the eye?"

She reached for Annette's cheeks and cradled her face in her hands. Annette squirmed ticklishly, but Thea sturdied her grip and held Annette's head still.

Eventually, Thea's and Annette's gazes met.

"Now, just stay right there."

They faced each other from about a foot apart.

One of Annette's eyes had an eye patch over it, but Thea was pretty sure that wouldn't be a problem. It should still work.

Thea pursed her lips.

Then a chill ran through her body. She had never felt anything like it before in her life.

Am I scared? Scared of finding out what Annette has in her heart?

The way Thea's heartbeat was accelerating was exactly like the physiological response to fear.

She didn't understand why, but her instincts were shouting at her not to get close to Annette.

No, no. This is no time to be backing down. I need to face my allies so I can butt heads with them.

Eventually, it was thoughts of her hero that allowed her to drive back her doubts.

It's the only way I can become like Ms. Hearth.

For three seconds, Thea peered into Annette's eyes—

"..What?"

—and arrived at a shocking conclusion.

"So?" Annette gave her a cherubic smile. "Didja see what was in my heart?"

Thea faltered for a moment. The desire she'd seen was so different from what she'd expected that she didn't know what to think. However, her technique had never led her astray before.

Really, though...?

Still, she couldn't believe it.

That's *what I can use to get Annette under control...?*

It took her a moment to figure out how to phrase it.

"U-um..." She swallowed, then spoke.

"Yes?"

"I've been thinking this for a while, but..."

It didn't make sense, but she had to at least try it.

"...did you get taller recently?"

Annette's face lit up like a flower bud blooming.

"Wow, Sis! You noticed?" She jumped at Thea and dangled off her neck. "I totally did, yo! I grew an eighth of an inch this past month. And three-quarters of an inch since last year! I'm shooting right up, and it's all thanks to my new sleeping style."

Apparently, that was the reason behind the suspension.

Annette gave Thea's back a few hard thumps as she frolicked merrily. Her glee was as innocent as a child's.

"..............."

However, Thea's feelings were much more mixed.

"I want to grow taller."

That was Annette's deepest desire.

Thea had just peered into Annette's heart, but she felt like she understood less about her than ever. As far as she could tell, Annette didn't have anything resembling a central guiding philosophy. Reading her mind was like reading a five-year-old's.

Annette's heart was empty.

However, Thea decided to set that aside for now. "Once we pass the test, I'll make you some milk pudding."

"Yo, that'll make me even taller!" Annette cheered as she happily agreed to help.

It had taken no small amount of doing, but Thea had finally gotten two of her teammates to work together with her.

Over in her room, she gave a rousing speech.

"All right, everyone! Let's pass this test!"

She got a pair of enthusiastic responses back.

"Yeah!" "Let's do it, yo!"

Erna and Annette stood side by side and raised their fists in the air.

Thea felt her eyes swim.

"What's wrong, Big Sis Thea...?" Erna asked. By now, she was completely comfortable around her.

"Oh, it's nothing. I was just thinking about how far we've come..."

""Hmm?""

Annette and Erna cocked their heads to the side.

For some reason, Thea felt as tired as if she'd gone through a grueling test already.

"Anyhow, I just discovered some valuable intel. Apparently, Lily's room used to belong to Inferno's old boss. I'll use that fact as bait to bring Teach there. Annette, your job is to set up a trap in Lily's room, and Erna, your job is to just barely slip past the trap and touch Teach's hand."

After laying out the plan, Thea clapped her hands together.

"Now, let's do this! It's time to show Teach what our teamwork is capable of!"

Annette and Erna headed to Lily's room, and Thea went looking for Klaus. She heard sounds coming from his private bathroom, so that must have been where he was. Was he taking a shower?

If so, she would have no choice but to wait for him to finish.

Fretting over the time they were going to lose, Thea rushed over to the private bathroom.

Then she got the idea to surprise him while he was changing. She flung the bathroom door open—

"There, all done."

—and found Monika in the changing room tapping Klaus's hand.

A satisfying clap rang out.

"Huh…?"

Thea stared at them with her mouth hanging agape.

Monika washed her hands in the changing room sink, then let out a small laugh. "Good work. Y'know, I could really go for some lunch right now."

"W-wait, hold on a minute! H-how?!" Thea grabbed Monika's arm in a panic. Her voice rose an octave. "And you, Teach—why did you just let her touch your hand like that?!"

She didn't understand any of what had just happened.

This was a challenge Thea had been planning to tackle as a group of three, and yet Monika had just completed it all on her own. And with considerable ease, at that.

"Hmm?" Klaus gave Thea a puzzled look. "Weren't you working together?"

"N-no, Monika just went off on her own…"

"Ah, I see. It all makes sense now."

Klaus nodded as though this meant something profound, but Thea still didn't get it. "How was Monika able to pass the test?"

"When a person goes about their day, there's one time where they invariably leave their hands defenseless. Monika realized that and capitalized on it." Klaus sounded almost dejected. "It's when they wash them."

Even after hearing that, Thea still didn't get it.

Monika had pulled off the incredible feat of landing a blow on the mighty Klaus. Thea understood that much, but that was all.

"It's really no big deal." Monika dried off her hands with a handkerchief. "It doesn't take some big plan to touch someone's hands. You just have to get in the way of them washing them. What really pissed me off is how you missed the golden opportunity."

"Wh-what do you mean?"

"Klaus was working with animals. People always wash their hands after that."

"Ah…"

"I even left you a hint. You saw that list of Heat Haze Palace faucets, right?" Monika's voice rang with pride.

As she spoke, Thea's memories turned.

"I broke the tap out in the garden ahead of time. Then I left Erna in the kitchen and sent Annette over to the washroom. The communal bath is girls only; Teach wasn't gonna go there. That meant Teach had nowhere to wash his hands but the sink in his private bathroom, so all I had to do was wait here."

Everything Thea had seen and heard that day flashed back through her mind.

There was the wrench she'd seen Monika holding out in the garden. There was the fact that she'd left Erna alone on cooking duty. There was the mysteriously broken faucet in the washroom that Annette had been working to fix.

Monika had been cutting off places for Klaus to wash his hands.

Having now finally reached a sink, Klaus began diligently washing his hands with soap. It was the natural thing to do; after all, he had just been handling mice with his bare hands.

"Remember what I told you? I have to get the mice to the handler by this afternoon. I didn't have time to waste dawdling, so I had no choice but to offer her my hand."

Klaus's only options were to drive the girls off without using his hands or give up. With time being of the essence, he had chosen the latter.

Monika gave Thea an overly familiar thump on the shoulder.

"Thanks. You made for a great diversion."

"A-a diversion…?"

"You totally went for that note I left in Lily's room, didn't you? It was a big help, you babysitting the kids like that."

Monika must have been eavesdropping on Thea and Klaus's conversation in the animal pen. Then she manipulated Thea and the others while she went in for the kill herself.

Thea flared up. She had been dancing on the palm of Monika's hand that whole time.

"C-come on! If that was your plan, you should have told us!"

"Excuse me? I think a little thanks are in order. Or better yet, an apology. You have anything you wanna say about telling me not to get in your way?"

"~~~~~!" Thea let out a soundless scream.

She wanted to shout at the top of her lungs that it didn't make sense, but no matter how she sliced it, Monika had a point. Thea couldn't get the words out. It stung. It *hurt*, and she didn't know what to do about it.

As she searched for what she wanted to say—

"Magnificent."

—she heard satisfaction in Klaus's voice.

"That'll do just fine."

He gave them a round of applause. Apparently, he was pleased with how things had turned out.

Thea cocked her head to the side. "It will? But we didn't end up working together at all…"

"Oh, I never thought for a moment that you four would be able to cooperate peacefully."

"That's horrible… I mean, you're right, but that's horrible!"

"As far as that department goes, our four absent members have you beat by a mile."

There was no arguing that point. Thea had little doubt that Lily's quartet was lifting each other up and taking on their mission as a team. She envied them. She wished she could be with *that* group.

"Spies with considerable skills often have considerable egos to match. I told Thea this earlier, but differences are the key to a strong team. What I expect out of you four is for you to strip each other's egos raw and cooperate by butting heads."

"So you're saying…"

"Thea, you tried to pull your teammates together and complete your task that way. Monika, you wrote teamwork off as useless and schemed to manipulate your teammates as efficiently as possible. Both of you did wonderful work—and both of you were magnificent." Klaus nodded. "Through antagonism, you reached your goal. That's how the five of us are going to take down Corpse."

A sigh of relief escaped Thea's lips. They were being allowed onto the mission.

Monika spoke up in the smuggest voice imaginable. "Good for you. You picked up my scraps; now you get to come on the mission."

"Rrgh..."

Monika was totally looking down on her. She was basically convinced that she was the only reason they'd passed the test. However, she wasn't totally wrong, so Thea had no choice but to grit her teeth and take it.

"Yo, Sis!"

As she did, Annette popped her head in from the hallway.

"We've been waiting for Klaus to show up for forever. Is he coming?"

Annette and Erna were still on standby.

The two of them had completely slipped Thea's mind.

"Oh, I'm sorry. Monika actually already passed the test."

"Boo. That's a bummer, yo." Annette gave her a smile. She didn't look disappointed in the slightest. "I already set it up so there're two doorknobs, and if you turn the wrong one, there's a huge explosion!"

"You're really fond of explosions, aren't you?"

Her trap sounded dangerous, so Thea wanted it disarmed ASAP.

Doubly so because it was on Lily's room. If anything happened to Hearth's old bedroom, Thea would have been heartbroken.

"I hate to have to ask, but could you disassemble your trap?"

"I want my milk pudding first."

"Come on, now, let's not be stubborn. The disassembly comes first. You wouldn't want your bomb to go off by accident, would you?"

"Objection! You'd have to be super unlucky to trigger the trap, yo."

That wasn't exactly the problem here, but Annette did sort of have a point.

Her handiwork was impeccable, and none of her inventions had ever malfunctioned. Plus, anyone who ran across a door that had abruptly grown a second knob would naturally approach it with caution. And even if they did try to open the door, they still had a fifty-fifty shot of emerging unscathed.

Despite all that, Thea still wanted Annette to remove the bomb, but—

"By the way, where's Erna?"

The moment the question left Klaus's mouth, a tremor shook the entire manor.

""""   """"
....

As a terrible explosion rocked their eardrums, black smoke began billowing toward them from down the hallway.

Thea rushed over to a window and threw it open. She looked out to check the situation. Fortunately, it didn't look like anything had caught fire.

The smoke gradually faded, and once the ventilation was complete, they all hurried over to check the scene.

The explosion had come from Lily's room. Erna lay before its blown-up door, her body pitch-black with soot.

"...How unlucky."

Well, at least she was alive.

It had taken her prodigious powers working overtime, but she'd survived.

"When I came back from the washroom, there was a second doorknob."

And so she turned one of them. The wrong one.

"And I don't know why, but...the washroom sink exploded, too..."

By the sound of it, she had eaten both blasts back-to-back.

When they peered in, they discovered that Lily's room was in rough shape. The window was a goner, of course, as was the outer wall it had been a part of. At least the view from the second floor was nice. The room's bed and dresser had gotten blasted all the way out into the garden, and the poison-filled vials Lily had been dutifully collecting lay shattered across the floor.

"Well, this is, um...a dilemma..." Thea found herself at a loss for words. Everything Lily owned had been blown to smithereens.

"The way I see it..." Monika crossed her arms. "...this is all Erna's fault for going and touching stuff when she knew her luck is so bad."

"Well, I think it's Annette's fault for going so overboard with the blasting powder!" Erna cried indignantly.

"I was just following Thea's orders, yo!"

"Wait, me?" Caught off guard by the sudden game of "pass the blame," Thea hurriedly denied Annette's accusation as well. "You know, if Monika had just cooperated with us from the get-go, I don't think that accident would have happened at all!"

"You are *not* pinning this on me," Monika snapped.

"Don't try to talk your way out of this. Just look at the sorrow in Teach's eyes!" Thea pointed at Klaus, who had yet to say a word. "A woman he cares about and misses dearly just got her room blown up. Can't you see the despair in his face?!"

"...................."

Klaus stood motionless. His expression was even more subdued than usual.

"It's okay." The words spilled quietly from his mouth. "I'm holding back the tears. Barely."

"Why, we've never even seen him this wounded!"

It felt wrong, hearing that coming from Klaus.

To make matters worse, he wasn't the only one who'd suffered an emotional wound from the sudden tragedy. Thea felt the exact same way.

Ms. Hearth's rooooom...

She had been planning on talking Lily into trading rooms with her, but now that plan had gone up in smoke.

"...Perhaps I ought to say something after all," Klaus remarked. "I won't ask that you get along, but...do at least *try* to work together."

His voice was hollow and lifeless. It must have taken everything he had to get the words out at all.

Interlude

Missing ①

"...and that's about it."

With that, Klaus finished telling his story.

Now everyone was up to speed on what he had seen the chosen members do, how they had trained before they went up against Corpse, and finally, how Lily's room ended up getting destroyed.

"""" .... """""

His audience of four didn't quite know what to make of that.

"They're somethin', all right." Sybilla scratched her head. "Something *crazy*, sure, but somethin'..."

Sara nodded. "They all have really strong personalities. It must have been a challenge, getting them to work together..."

"They were a bit of a handful, yes." Klaus crossed his arms and sighed.

Although Thea was technically the one who had united the four girls, Klaus's work had been cut out for him anyway. Due to Thea's incessant breakdowns, she had needed just as much hand-holding as the others.

"All that aside, though, their skills are no joke. We finished the mission itself without a hitch."

"Yeah, well, if they're really that talented, they wouldn't have blown up my room!" After ranting and raving for a little while, Lily cleared her throat. "Someone's gonna pay for that later, but for now... We still don't know why they haven't called, huh?"

The other girls nodded.

Even after laying out all the facts, they still weren't any closer toward solving their missing persons case.

Why hadn't the others returned to Heat Haze Palace yet?

Why hadn't they at least given Klaus a call?

Mysteries abounded.

Klaus gave the order. "We're going looking for them. You all, go on ahead. I have another mission I need to finish, but I'll follow along after I'm done."

He stood up from the sofa and made for his room. Even in circumstances like theirs, he couldn't just up and leave at a moment's notice. Being the strongest spy in the country was a role that carried heavy responsibilities.

However, one of his pupils didn't agree. "I don't think that's wise…" Grete gave her calm, reasoned argument in a moderate tone. "For all we know, every second might matter. I think you should join the search immediately, Boss."

Klaus shook his head. "I would if I could, but this mission has civilian lives on the line. I can't put it off."

"Then let me take it on for you so you can go to Thea and the others."

This time, Grete's voice rang with pride. After all, they'd finished their last mission without needing his help.

Even so, there was no way he could have her assume the mission alone…

Sybilla and Sara rose to their feet to back Grete up.

"I'll stay, too," Sybilla said. "My wound's all better. You go on and make sure the others are okay."

"I—I don't know how much help I'll be, but I'll do what I can here, too," agreed Sara.

Having secured her teammates' assistance, Grete gave Klaus a small smile. "You needn't worry, Boss. Even without you, we were still able to best Corpse's disciple, and if we think we're in any danger, we'll back out immediately."

"…You've grown."

A month ago, they had caused him nothing but worry. He would never have even dreamed of letting girls that inexperienced take on a mission solo.

Now, though, he could make that decision without a moment's hesitation.

"Magnificent. Very well, then. The mission is yours."

If that wasn't praiseworthy, he didn't know what was.

"Thank you... Just as I expected."

Seeing her teammates' determination threw Lily for a loop for a moment. The words got caught in her throat. "Ah, erm, I..."

"Lily, you're with me," Klaus declared. "The two of us will be following our teammates' tracks."

"Y-yes, sir!"

Understanding how much she cared about her team, Klaus knew she wanted to rush to their side as soon as possible.

It made more sense to take her along than to leave her behind.

"It's time for an emergency mission. Our job is to find the others and bring them back alive."

And with that, Klaus and Lily left Heat Haze Palace.

Chapter 2

Reunion

It was four days before Klaus and Lily would set off on their search-and-rescue mission.

Thea lay on her deck chair looking as comfortable as could be. She was dressed in a black swimsuit created with a titillatingly small amount of fabric.

The sun had already set, leaving the outdoor pool to be lit by a series of purple lights. However, the lighting wasn't particularly strong, and even combined with the glow of the hotel towering beside it, it was still rather dim. There must have also been lights installed on the bottom of the pool, as a reddish-purple hue glimmered on its surface and helped accentuate the sinful atmosphere permeating the scene.

She was in the entertainment district located on the southernmost tip of the Din Republic.

In days of yore, a gold vein was discovered in a nearby mountain. Workers were brought in from all over, and they even set up a railway system. Then, once the vein ran dry, they invested their money into building tourist attractions there to prevent it from becoming a ghost town. Nowadays, it was the hottest destination spot in all of Din. There were underground casinos on every corner, and the wealthy and powerful were no doubt gambling mind-boggling sums of money at that very moment.

The city had even avoided suffering major damages in the Great War, and its lights never went out.

At the moment, Thea was relaxing at the pool of one of the city's luxury hotels.

We did just complete that mission, after all. I think I've earned a little indulgence.

It was just after they had completed their mission to take out Corpse.

On Klaus's instructions, they had gone to the city where the assassin was hiding and captured him in brilliant form. Afterward, they had traced Corpse's path to see if they could find anything on any collaborators of his, and now they were here.

Though, if I'm being honest, Teach did at least 90 percent of the work...

The girls' responsibilities had been minimal. In fact, basically all they'd done was clear the area of civilians during the battle. They had contributed a little in rooting out the assassin's hiding spot, but Klaus had carried out the capture more or less on his own.

And what's more, the four of us were never really able to get on the same page...

They had performed their individual tasks just fine, but their teamwork never ended up coming together.

If Klaus hadn't given them orders in the exacting detail he had, they would never have been able to pull through.

As Thea stood up to distract herself from the painful memories, someone showed up beside her.

"What the hell's wrong with this place?"

It was Monika. She was technically wearing a swimsuit as well, but she had a jacket on over hers. She made no efforts to hide her displeasure as she glared at the pool.

"Why's there outside heating? Why's the pool open in the middle of the night? What's with the sleazy lighting?"

"It's a luxury hotel. Have you not been to one before?"

"Of course not. Why would I?"

"Heh-heh. We *did* just finish that mission, you know. What's the point, if you don't treat yourself at times like these?"

"God, you're even soft on yourself."

Monika's words were harsh, but the truth of the matter was that the completion bonuses they got for successful spy missions were lavish, and how they spent their money was up to them.

I swear... Ever since day one, Monika's just been picking one fight after another.

She gave Monika a withering look, but Monika just ignored her.

Instead, she sat down on a deck chair and started reading. Surprisingly enough, her book of choice was a romance novel. Perhaps due to the poor lighting, her eyebrows were furrowed.

"Ugh... If Klaus hadn't ordered us to stick together, I can promise you I'd be anywhere but here right now."

"I won't tell if you don't."

Monika and Thea weren't exactly spending their vacations together by choice. No, there was a specific reason they were staying at the same hotel.

"Oh yeah? Then, who'd watch the kids?" Thea looked back over at the pool.

"Time for my super-special upgraded squirt gun, yo!"

"What?!"

In the water, Annette was carrying a massive squirt gun, and Erna was desperately trying to swim away.

At first glance, they looked like a pair of kids just playing around... but it was a little too intense for that description to really capture it.

"Charging up!" Annette cranked her squirt gun's handle, and it began sucking in water from the pool. "Fire at will, yo!" A loud blast rang out as a huge burst of water struck Erna square in the face.

"...Is she okay?" Thea wondered aloud. "I can't tell if Erna is keeping her head above water or not."

"If you're that worried, just go help her."

"If I tried that, what do you think would happen?"

"Oh yeah, I guess the little monster would switch targets to you."

"...I think I'll stay out of this one."

"Yeah, same."

For once, the two of them agreed on something.

They felt for Erna, but Annette needed *someone* to keep her occupied.

Klaus had left them with instructions to all stay at the same hotel, as it was important that somebody keep an eye on Erna and Annette. If the two were left to their own devices, trouble was certain to find them.

Over to the side, they heard Erna moan "How unlucky..." as she suffered a personal flash flood.

"You've noticed it, too, right?" Monika asked. "Annette's tech is more advanced than anything Din's got."

"I did come to the same conclusion, yes."

"Where the hell is she from?"

Where *did* their mysterious amnesiac teammate grow up?

It was a good question, but Monika had meant it rhetorically. She looked down at her book and resumed reading.

"Why not take advantage of the opportunity and go for a swim? You can read anywhere, can't you?" Thea asked.

"Watch yourself," Monika replied. "You talk bad about reading on vacation, you're gonna make enemies of every bookworm in the world."

"We have to go back in just three days, though... Say, let's hit a casino after Erna and Annette go to bed. Think how unbeatable we'd be if the two of us teamed up."

"I'm plenty unbeatable on my own." Monika's attitude was as chilly as ever.

Even now that they'd completed their mission, she still didn't show any signs of wanting to play nice.

"Why are you being such an ass?! I'm offering you an olive branch here!"

"Maybe some of us don't like getting olive branches constantly shoved in our faces."

"Tch. You know, maybe you and I *do* need to settle things. Shall we have it out?"

"Hey, Annette. Give the slut a taste of your water gun."

"Wait, that's cheating!"

Sensing the imminent danger she was in, Thea yelped—

"——!"

—then heard a woman's voice calling for someone. That much made sense; it was a nice hotel, so it was no surprise that there would be other guests there.

Then Annette screamed.

"Ack!"

When Thea looked up, she saw a woman diving into the pool, fully clothed, and wrapping Annette in a head-on embrace.

Thea moved fast. Something serious was going down.

She hurried toward the interloper, then stood imposingly by the poolside and gave her a steely glare. "Who're you?"

The woman was short and had big, bright eyes. She was probably in her midthirties. Her long, wispy hair and pallid skin gave her a sort of sickly aura, and the way her soaked gray blouse clung to her body only made the impression worse.

"I, um..."

The woman was still holding Annette close as she spoke.

"...I'm her mother."

None of them had seen that one coming.

It was a reunion that could only be described as miraculous—a stroke of destiny that not even Klaus had anticipated.

It also marked the beginning of the end.

Without so much as pausing to give Klaus time to reach them, the team began unraveling at the seams.

Interlude

Missing ②

Klaus and Lily were riding in a private compartment on their train.

The good news was that they knew where their missing colleagues had gone to do their sightseeing—the entertainment district in the southernmost part of Din. The area had largely avoided the ravages of war, and even now, it felt like new hotels were going up every day. Underground casinos ran rampant there, as did the gangs that controlled them.

As seedy as its underbelly was, though, the legal entertainment options were all perfectly safe, and the city was a popular destination spot for foreign tourists.

When their train arrived at its first station, Klaus got off to stop by the station kiosk and purchase a newspaper and a cigar. Lily regarded him with surprise as he returned to their compartment.

"You smoke, Teach?"

"No, I put in a request to the brass. This station was the drop site."

Klaus unrolled the cigar and withdrew the report from inside it. He skimmed it over, then handed it to Lily.

"You should read this, too. It's the intel we have on the city."

"You got it... Uh, Teach, this is a recipe for corn soup."

"It's a cipher. It's fine; I'll read it off to you." Klaus already had the report memorized, and he recited it for her. "Five days ago, a spy battle took place there. The clash was between the Lylat Kingdom and the Galgad Empire, and Din had no direct involvement. Our understanding is that the heart of the matter revolved around a Lylat politician who was conducting a foreign inspection."

"I take it that 'inspection' was just an excuse to visit the entertainment district?" Lily remarked.

"Probably, and it gave the Empire a chance to attack him," Klaus replied. "When local police caught wind of the battle, they got in touch with our army. The army responded by going into high alert and blockading the area so they could catch the operatives who had infiltrated our borders. The Lylat spy's corpse has already been found, but the Imperial spy is still at large and trying to flee as we speak."

Lily's eyes grew wider with every word. "Wait, so you mean Thea and the others are in a total powder keg right now?"

"That about sums it up, yes. I shouldn't have been so careless." Klaus sighed, then splashed some mineral water on the report.

The liquid caused the report to dissolve. In no time at all, it was gone without a trace.

"The army delayed their report to us on purpose. They wanted to make sure they were the ones who got all the credit."

Because of that, Klaus hadn't known anything about the spy battle going down at their destination. If he had, he would've told the girls to choose a different site for their vacation.

Lily tilted her head to the side, not fully satisfied.

"Okay, so backing up a few steps…"

"Yes?"

"Why don't we and the rest of the Foreign Intelligence Office get along better with the army? We're all on the same side, aren't we? I remember that the virus leak happened because they developed it in secret, too."

Apparently, her spy academy hadn't filled her in on the complicated relationship between the two organizations.

Perhaps he had better explain. It wasn't like there was anything else they could do until the train reached its destination, after all.

"It ties back to the way we were founded, I suppose. Back before the war, our intelligence agency was split into two branches—the Military Intelligence Department and the Naval Intelligence Department. The military handled enemy spies lurking within our borders, and the navy specialized in gathering information abroad, but they both liked to keep secrets to themselves, and it led to our nation underperforming on the intelligence front."

"Well, *that* doesn't sound familiar or anything…"

"Because of that, Din founded a new intelligence agency that could cover the duties of both branches. That was how we got the Foreign Intelligence Office that we have today."

"Ooh," Lily cooed in delight. "That's kinda cool! Like, *voom*! Combine!"

"Indeed. From what I understand, they took the best and the brightest from both departments."

"Nice, nice…"

"In short, they made an elite organization with nothing but the cream of the crop. And that's why the army hates us."

"Wh—?" Lily's expression went stiff. "That's it?!"

"That's it."

"Wh-what're they, kids?"

"To be more specific, it's because of how radically different we are in scope. Compared to the hundreds of thousands of people in the military, the Foreign Intelligence Office only has a few thousand members at most. Furthermore, we take all the vast amounts of information the army and navy gather and examine it behind closed doors. You could certainly look at it as us using them as our errand boys."

When you got down to brass tacks, the Foreign Intelligence Office's salaries were higher, too. That much was somewhat inevitable, given that any able-bodied adult could join the army, whereas you had to be selected by a scout to become a spy. That was another reason behind the bad blood.

"Well now, that's hardly our fault! Ugh! Now *I'm* starting to get ticked off!"

Lily's body began trembling more and more violently.

When she couldn't take it anymore, she thrust her fist into the air.

"We need to spread the word about our grand accomplishments! The military let their bioweapon fall into the wrong hands, and we spies were the ones who brilliantly got it ba— OWWW!" Klaus kicked her shin to shut her up.

"Don't go blabbing state secrets like that."

If word got out that they'd been developing bioweapons, they would come under fire from the international community for it. Even among their own army, only a small handful of people knew exactly what had gone down.

"In all seriousness, you can hate the army all you want, but make sure you don't underestimate them."

"Ooh, I do like the sound of hating them…"

"There are two areas where their strength vastly exceeds ours: hierarchy and manpower."

The army's value was in its sheer numbers.

Some tasks that were beyond even the greatest spies could be achieved if you threw enough bodies at the problem.

"Only the army has the ability to blockade an entire city like this. The enemy spy is surrounded, and they're probably at their wit's end. They might even tear the city apart in desperation."

"Excuse me, *what*?"

"Sometimes, a cornered spy will start massacring people as an all-or-nothing attempt to get free. It's rare, but it does happen."

Lily went pale.

Klaus nodded. That was simply a sign of how powerful the army's ability to overwhelm their foe with sheer numbers was.

"If that happens, all we can do is pray that our teammates don't get caught up in the middle of it."

The train started up again and began picking up speed.

Klaus glanced at the scenery outside the window. It didn't take long after leaving the station for the ocean to come into view. Just beyond the curving shoreline, he could make out a group of hotels.

"But if I'm being honest…we probably can't afford to turn a blind eye to a domestic incident like this."

If their allies were in danger, that would naturally take priority, but there was something still smoldering within Klaus.

His mind was consumed with thoughts of the mysterious Imperial group Serpent.

He needed to start investigating as soon as possible. Even setting his personal vendetta aside, it was a key national security issue for the Din Republic as a whole.

Klaus needed to find the mastermind responsible for this mess and give them hell.

Chapter 3

Mother and Daughter

Thea walked out to the balcony and let the cool sea breeze wash over her flush skin.

The hem of her negligee fluttered.

She took a sip of the iced tea she'd ordered from room service. The pleasant taste of Darjeeling filling her mouth didn't just cool her body; it helped calm her heart, too.

The night skyline lay spread out before her. Hotels sat clustered together, their flickering lights making them look like single massive giants. She doubted you could find anywhere else in the Republic with a view that impressive.

Over on the other side of the balcony, Monika was using a reading light to thumb through a novel. Next to her, there was a stack of other books over a dozen titles high. She clearly intended to spend her entire vacation reading. Every book in the pile was a by-the-numbers romance novel where young men and woman met and fell deeply in love.

Monika snapped at Thea before the latter even had a chance to speak. "It's intellectual curiosity, that's all. It's not like I'm actually into this boy-meets-girl stuff."

"What? I didn't say anything."

"You had a look your eyes."

"Well, I suppose you have me there."

"Also," Monika said, still mostly focused on her book, "put some clothes on before you come out here."

"Why? It's not like anyone's looking."

"I'm here, aren't I?"

"Hmm-hmm. I could come out naked, if you'd rather?"

"...I hate you so much."

After assuring Monika that she was just kidding, Thea sat down in the chair beside hers.

Monika snapped her book shut in annoyance. "What? Is this about Matilda?"

"Erna and Annette are asleep now, so I wanted to ask how you really feel."

"I *feel* like we should've ditched her. It's not like Annette remembers her or anything." She gave Thea a reproachful glare. "So why'd you have to go and make that stupid promise?"

Sure enough, Monika was against it.

Thea thought back to the promise she'd made to Annette's mom...

The woman had introduced herself as Matilda.

She was an engineer from the neighboring Lylat Kingdom, and according to her business card, she worked for a company that produced heavy machinery. Thea recognized the name. The company hadn't been around for long, but it was a major corporation known globally for its high-quality work. They also had a robust warranty program where they would send out engineers from their headquarters in Lylat to personally deal with any equipment that broke down.

Matilda was one such engineer. She had come to the hotel to fix its fountain, and by the sound of it, she was no stranger to the Din Republic.

"I took her with me to visit the Republic four years ago, but we got in a train accident. They took me to the hospital, but they couldn't find her anywhere..."

Thea and the other three girls sat by the poolside table as Matilda told them her story. Matilda knew about a mole on the back of Annette's neck, and when they looked, they could definitely see the resemblance between the two of them. It appeared she was telling the truth about being Annette's mom.

Miraculous as the reunion was, though, Thea found herself having mixed feelings about the whole thing.

"I had no idea she was still alive. You see, her actual name is—"

Matilda said a name Thea didn't recognize, but apparently, that was Annette's real name.

The person in question tilted her head. "Who's that? I don't get it, yo."

"What...?" Matilda's eyes went wide with shock.

"Annette," Thea said, "why don't you go play with Erna?"

"Now that, I get!"

Annette wrapped her arm around Erna's neck and grinned. "Erna, let's go play with squirt guns!" she crowed as she dragged the unfortunate blond toward the pool. Erna's despair-filled eyes stood in sharp contrast to Annette's gleeful expression. "Please, no. Please, someone save me...," she begged.

Thea felt sorry for her, but she chose to ignore her pleas.

Once the conversation's subject was gone, Thea began explaining. "So to make a long story short...she has amnesia."

She kept her story simple and mixed in lies where she needed to.

It wasn't clear why, but Annette couldn't remember anything from more than four years back. In Thea's version of events, she had been given the name Annette when she was taken in as a ward of the state. From there, she was transferred to a religious boarding school, and Thea and the others were her friends who were out on vacation together.

After laying it all out, she went on. "I'm really sorry, ma'am, but Annette doesn't remember anything about her mother."

Matilda covered her mouth with her hands. "It can't be..."

"Also, we can't just nod along and hand her over to you. Not to be rude or anything, but we don't have any actual proof that you're her mother, and we would have to talk it over with the school before we did anything anyway."

Matilda hung her head. The situation had finally sunk in. "...So you're telling me that my daughter lost her memories in that train accident and has been living a whole different life since then?"

Thea wasn't sure what to say to her.

As far as the law went, the Din Republic would have to return Annette to her mother if Matilda could prove the two of them were related. However, that was only the legal side of the story.

What they *really* needed to consider was what Annette wanted.

"…Even just getting to see her alive like this feels like a blessing from the heavens." At that point, Matilda finally smiled. "She seems happy, and that means the world to me."

She looked lovingly at Annette as she frolicked about in the pool. Annette's teary-eyed companion didn't even register to her.

Fortunately for them, Matilda didn't seem like she was going to assert her parental rights and take Annette from them by force.

She seemed like a quiet, reserved woman—the exact opposite of her brash "Yo"-spouting daughter.

Thea spoke up again. "Has Annette always been such a wild child?"

"Oh, absolutely. I can't count how many times she sneaked into my workshop and started tinkering with the machines. I didn't even teach her how, but she took to them like a natural. It was a bit of a headache at the time, but now those are some of my fondest memories."

"Ah, so that's where she picked up her skills…"

It all made sense. Sure enough, Annette *had* picked up her engineering know-how abroad.

"Thea," Monika interjected. "We gotta go. The pool's closing soon."

That was a lie. It was open for another two hours.

However, Thea could tell from the piercing look Monika was giving her that she wanted to cut the conversation short.

Thea suggested to Matilda that they exchange contact information. Matilda was hesitant at first—"I'm afraid it's not a very nice hotel…"—but she eventually gave in. It turned out that the rate of her hotel room was less than a tenth of what Thea's was. It was no wonder she was a little embarrassed about it.

"Please!" As they parted ways, Matilda grabbed Thea by the hand. "I know this is selfish to ask, but would it be possible for me to have dinner with my daughter tomorrow night?"

"T-tomorrow…?"

"I want to do what little I can to fill in the four years we've lost. Please, is there any way you can help me?"

She clenched Thea's hand in hers and laid on the pressure. Thea had no way to escape.

Maternal love was a powerful thing.

She was a bit worried about the way Monika was glaring at her—

"…Of course. I'll go ahead and make a reservation for the two of you."

—but she didn't see any choice but to go ahead and nod.

"Oh, thank you so much."

Matilda gave Thea a deep bow and shook Thea's hands with astounding vigor.

Monika clicked her tongue. The noise echoed in Thea's ear.

Thea let out a long sigh as she recalled what had happened.

"What was I supposed to do? Turn her down and ruin that heart-stirring reunion?"

"Heart-stirring? Not to Annette, it wasn't."

"Well, what would you have said to her?"

Monika put on a show of thinking for a few seconds. "'You've got the wrong person. Leave us alone, or I'm calling the cops.'"

"That's horrible!"

"'I gave birth to her myself. She couldn't possibly be your daughter.'"

"My, what a twist that would be."

"'Yeah, we get this a lot—crazy fans trying to get in with our actresses by pretending to be their estranged mothers.'"

"Please don't go giving Annette any weird backstories."

"The point is: You should've turned her down." After finishing her odd skit, Monika shrugged. "She wants to take Annette away from us. You get how dangerous that is, don't you?"

Thea reflexively glanced back over her shoulder.

On the bed, Annette was sleeping like a log. She'd given up on sleeping suspended, but her bedtime posture was no better than before. One of her legs was stretched all the way to the next bed over, and she was kicking Erna in the face.

"You want to let her quit Lamplight?"

"⋯⋯⋯⋯⋯⋯"

Thea had considered the possibility.

If Matilda ended up taking Annette back home with her, Annette wouldn't be able to stay with Lamplight anymore. She would end up leaving the world of spies behind her and living an ordinary life as a citizen of Lylat.

"Look, that's obviously off the table." Monika laughed triumphantly. "The team needs her. Even I have to give her credit, you know?"

She pulled something out of her pocket—a pair of completely identical tawny-brown long wallets.

"It's a perfect replica." She gave one of the wallets a shake, and three small balls dropped out. "It only took her one glance at my wallet to make this. It looks exactly like what you can buy off the shelf, but it's got a trick to it. If you give it a little flick, it shoots out these bouncy balls. They're a throwing weapon made of metal coated in rubber, and thanks to this, I can carry three of them around with me in a normal old wallet."

Annette had inherited that engineering prowess from Matilda.

However, would engineering skills alone have been enough to build a copy that perfect?

"That must have taken incredible recall ability," Thea noted.

"Pretty ironic, having an amnesiac with a great memory. She memorized what it looked like in a single glance, then made a weapon that appeared identical. That's a damn powerful trick."

Thea shared Monika's opinion.

Annette was an invaluable member of Lamplight. They couldn't afford to lose her.

"By the way," Monika asked, "what's the girl of the hour think about all this?"

"She said she was 'fine with whatever, yo.'"

Thea had explained the situation to Annette as impartially as she could, and Annette's response had been tepid at best. She hadn't shown a shred of interest toward her mother.

As far as Annette was concerned, Matilda was just some stranger to her.

"Then that settles it." Monika clapped her hands together. "Screw the promise. We're bailing before that woman can put any weird ideas in Annette's—"

"But the way I see it—this could be a good opportunity for Annette."

"Excuse me?"

"I'm going keep the promise and let Matilda and Annette meet again tomorrow."

A grim expression flashed across Monika's face. Her eyes burned with a mixture of disbelief and scorn. "Why? They're just going to get split up again. What good will letting them get closer do?"

"………"

"Unless, what, you're seriously thinking of handing her over?"

Thea shook her head. That wasn't it.

She knew she was being indecisive, but she couldn't bring herself to believe that tearing that mother and daughter apart was the right thing to do.

"She was empty."

"What?"

"That's what I felt when I looked into Annette's heart. There was nothing there. No reason for wanting to be a spy—and no reason to stay with Lamplight. All she operates on are pleasure and displeasure."

Thea was the only one who'd seen into Annette's heart, so only she could understand just how eerie it was to find nothing but that simple, childish desire.

"I want to grow taller."

"I don't know about you, but I think that's pretty twisted. When we go on missions, we're putting our lives on the line. But the thing is: She doesn't have any memories or sense of purpose. Letting someone like her risk her life just to satisfy her curiosity doesn't sit right with me. She... How do I put it? I want her to have a better foundation than that."

She thought back to how Annette had replied when the team reunited, how she'd acted back when they all stood in front of Inferno's grave, and all the times she had said that being with them was "fun." In retrospect, it all felt so dangerously noncommittal.

"You and I really don't see eye to eye, do we?" There was a harsh edge to Monika's voice. "I don't give a rat's ass about my teammates' personal lives. The good of the team should come first."

In other words, she felt that what the group needed should take priority over its members' feelings.

That was a perfectly legitimate way of looking at things—a very Monika way of looking at things.

"I'm not asking you to help," Thea replied. "All you have to do is sit back and watch."

"Oh yeah?"

"If you think my last reason was hypocritical, then let me rephrase. Don't you think it would serve Lamplight's interests if Annette found a proper motive for wanting to be a spy?"

As Annette was now, she was so inscrutable it made her impossible to control.

"………"

Monika went silent. She gazed out at the city lights, then spoke with some reluctance. "...Fine, do what you want. If it'll help keep her in line, I won't get in your way."

"I appreciate it."

Half-hearted as it was, Thea had Monika's seal of approval. That was a big relief.

Then Monika raised two fingers. "I've got two conditions."

"Do tell."

"I'm coming to the dinner, too. I need to make sure you don't get any funny ideas about handing over Annette."

"That's fine. And the other?"

"Strictly speaking, this is more of a request than a condition."

Monika exasperatedly jabbed her thumb at their two teammates inside the room.

"You need to stay with those two and make sure they don't embarrass me."

"GRAAAAH! Quit trying to run away! I picked it for you myself!"

"But I hate it, yo. It makes me look like a kid."

"Shaddap! Nobody asked what you want!"

Annette tried her best to flee, but Monika dragged her back kicking and screaming.

They were in their suite, and Monika was on a rampage of epic proportions. The first thing she'd done that morning was call up a clothing store and had them bring over their entire catalog of dresses. When they did, she chose one on the spot and tried to get Annette into it.

The dress suited her; that much was unmistakable. However, its pastel color and frilly design weren't to her liking, causing it to earn a rare display of resistance out of her.

"I'm a mature adult lady, so I wanna wear something cooler!"

Despite Annette's insistence, though, Monika showed no mercy. She pinned her teammate down on the bed, stripped off her pajamas, and shoved her into the dress by force.

Thea started to feel kind of bad for Annette.

"You know, Monika... I don't see why you can't just let her wear something she likes..."

"Because she'll pick out something horrible, that's why." Monika shot her suggestion down flatly. "If Annette goes out there looking like a mess, it'll reflect badly on us as her friends."

"Th-this is about your pride?"

"God dammit, sit still already. We could've been done here two hours ago."

The look on Monika's face was downright bloodcurdling as she finally wrestled Annette into her dress. Annette kicked her legs back and forth. "That tickles, yo!" It was impossible to tell if she was complaining or enjoying herself.

Over to the side, Erna was wearing a classic black dress and watching their battle in terror. Monika's heavy-handed behavior had given her such a fright that she'd tucked herself away in a corner of the room. "I—I...I'll go make breakfast. We have that bread and jam we bought yesterday..."

"Don't you move an inch," Monika snapped.

"The jam went flying all over my clothes!"

"That was quick, even for you." Monika's tone was tinged with annoyance. She clicked her tongue. "Thea, go wash Erna's dress. I want it back here and clean in five minutes."

"...Whatever you say, *ma'am*."

Monika had been like that all day, giving the others instructions detailed down to the minute. Every so often, she would end up shouting at them.

"We're going there to size her up. Don't you realize she'll be doing the same thing?"

That was what she'd barked when she woke them all up at five in the morning. Then she got to work preparing outfits and giving them crash courses in table manners so they could avoid embarrassing themselves at the fancy restaurant they were going to.

Thea sighed as she dried Erna's dress. "You know, I can definitely see why you didn't fit in at your academy."

"I *told you*, I was half-assing it on purpose."

That was the one point she refused to cede.

In the end, their preparations took up nearly the entire day.

By the time they got to the hotel lobby and called for their taxi, the sun was already making its descent.

"Come on, let's go. And don't you dare let your clothes get dirty on the way there. That means you, Erna."

"The sunset is too bright..." When they got to the taxi stand, Erna squinted. "I need to avoid it."

"What did I *just* say?! What do you think you're doing, beelining straight for that puddle?!"

Monika grabbed Erna by the scruff of her neck and hurled her into the cab.

After a long series of trials and tribulations, Thea and the others finally reached their destination.

The restaurant sat right on the coastline, and the sea-facing wall was made entirely of glass, giving a beautiful view of the sunset. Its interior and tablecloths were almost dazzlingly white. Thea had pored over the guidebook so she could pick out the perfect spot.

Matilda was waiting patiently for them inside, just as arranged. She was wearing the same casual blouse as the day prior, and when she saw them, she bowed. "Ah, hello again."

Thea gave her an elegant smile and guided the group into the dining area. "Annette and Matilda, you two are at that table there."

She had called ahead and made sure to reserve two tables.

Matilda froze. "W-we aren't all together...?"

"Hmm? No, I thought you two would like to have some time to yourselves."

"Y-yes, I suppose you're right. I'll do my best."

For some reason, she seemed tense.

The whole intent behind the dinner was so Matilda and Annette could spend some time together. Thea knew that if the two tables were joined, they'd just be getting in the way.

She, Monika, and Erna headed to their own table.

"Now we wait," Thea said. "One side might have amnesia, but they're still family. I'm interested to see what we can learn from what she and Annette talk about."

"Yeah...assuming they talk at all," Monika replied.

Their table was a little ways away from Matilda and Annette's.

On Monika's insistence, Annette was wearing her hair down. She usually kept it sloppily tied up, but now it hung down straight with the curls blown out so as to play up her natural charm. She was a perfect, adorable beauty. Just so long as she didn't talk. Or move.

The hope was that Matilda would compliment her hair and dress, and that would help get the conversation rolling, but—

" .... "

" .... "

—instead, they just sat in silence for a terribly long time.

Matilda fidgeted with her hands as she stared at Annette.

Annette sat vacantly with a thin smile plastered on her face.

" .... "

" .... "

After another protracted silence, Matilda finally broke the ice.

"So…Annette? That's what you're called now, right?"

"Yup."

"Have you been well? You haven't been hurt or sick, have you?"

"I've been fine, yo."

"Oh, that's so good to hear. I've been thinking about you ever since last night, you know. It's been four whole years. I was worried sick that you might have contracted a disease or something."

"Oh, hey, me too."

"You were worried about me, too? That's so sweet to—"

"No, *my* health."

" .... "

" .... "

" .... "

" .... "

Monika tilted her head. "Huh? What's wrong with them?" she asked quietly.

"They're nervous. I totally get how they feel," Erna whispered back.

Thea spoke optimistically. "I think they'll be getting more comfortable around each other soon, though."

The appetizers and soup showed up shortly thereafter, but that didn't do the conversation any good.

Matilda simply ate in silence, not so much as commenting on the food. Annette, for her part, completely disregarded the table manners Monika had drilled into her and picked up her bowl to chug down her soup. However, her mother didn't so much as scold her.

Then the fish came out, and it was Annette's turn to speak up.

"I don't like this fish, yo."

"...But why?"

"It's got a defiant look in its eyes."

"But you used to love fish. You ate it all the time simmered in tomato sauce with shellfi—"

"I don't remember that."

"O-oh, right... Well, if you don't want to eat it, you certainly don't have to."

"I just hate its eyes. I never said I wasn't gonna eat it."

"........................."

"........................."

"..."

"..."

"It's kind of scary how out of sync they are," Erna murmured.

Monika agreed. "I'm getting secondhand anxiety just listening to them."

Thea squeezed her fists tight. "L-let's give them a little longer. Maybe they just need some time."

In what seemed like no time at all, the lamb steak main course came out.

The moment Thea took her first bite, she couldn't help but exclaim, "This is fantastic!" No matter how glum someone felt, eating something that delicious would be sure to evoke a reaction. And yet—

"..."

"..."

—just like before, Matilda and Annette ate in silence.

Halfway through the meal, Annette got up and went toward them. "Erna, gimme half your meat."

Erna trembled. "She's coming to shake me down..." Aside from that, though, Annette said nothing.

"..."

"..."

The long, long silence continued all the way up until dessert.

Monika sneered as she munched on her bread. "Looks like Mom's given up on even talking to her."

"You're horrible, you know that? After watching that, your first thought is about how to keep Annette?" Thea protested reflexively, although Monika had a point.

Sure, Thea could probably go over there and get the conversation flowing. However, having a third party step in to push things along would defeat the entire point.

The whole idea behind the dinner was to give mother and child a chance to see each other one-on-one.

Thea had gone out of her way to set the whole thing up, but it looked like her efforts had been for naught.

"I suppose you're right, though. Once our dessert comes, we should—"

She was going to say *Just go ahead and get going.*

Before she could, though, Erna's nose twitched.

Nothing got by Monika. "Erna?"

"...I can smell misfortune."

She had already figured out the source, too. She surreptitiously pointed at the entrance.

"We're surrounded."

Thea shot Monika a signal with her eyes.

Using the last of her steak sauce, she drew a map on her plate of their escape route and the formation they would take.

Monika gave her a disapproving frown, but she tossed her something under the table all the same.

The transceiver landed perfectly in Thea's lap. As she hid it in a handkerchief, she rose from her seat and headed for the other table.

"Matilda, we're going to pretend to use the toilet and sneak out the back."

When Thea whispered in her ear, Matilda looked at her with a start. She seemed to realize that something was up.

The restaurant had grown crowded, and they used that to their advantage to move stealthily across the room. There was a male waiter blocking the back exit, so Thea pretended to be drunk and flirted with him to divert his attention. As she did, she shot Matilda the go-ahead with her eyes and gave her an opportunity to slip outside.

From there, Thea headed to the bathroom for real and escaped out the window.

"There are three suspicious guys out front." Monika's voice crackled

through the transceiver. *"They realized you weren't coming back. They're on the move."*

"Can you tell who they are?"

"No one good, that's for sure. Now hurry, or they'll catch you. You've got forty seconds left."

Thea scanned her surroundings.

The restaurant sat on the coastline, and it was far enough from the hotels that they'd had to take a taxi to get there. Escaping out the back was only the first step. Now they needed to contend with the fact that they had the sizable highway on one side of them and a cliff face that towered above them like a castle's ramparts on the other. That much made sense, given that the region was sandwiched between a mountain and the sea, but it meant they had nowhere to hide.

"Monika, can you get them off our tail?"

"I could, but it'd be a bad move. I don't want to make a scene right next to the restaurant."

Monika could drive off any but the most trained of opponents. However, making a commotion in public like that was an absolute last resort.

"For now, follow the cliffside and head toward the ringing sound."

"The what?"

"Just do it."

Thea circled around to the back exit and joined up with Matilda, who looked as pale as a sheet. Thea pulled her along by the arm. As she ran, her thoughts turned.

Should I try to negotiate with them? No, given the situation, that's far too risky...

The highway was almost empty of cars, and Thea headed across it toward the light from the hotels.

"They're over there! Don't let 'em get away!"

She could hear a group of adults shouting angrily and running toward them from behind. They sounded murderous. If nothing else, they clearly weren't going to let her and Matilda escape without a fight.

Thea didn't know what they were after, but she didn't plan on sticking around to find out. "A little faster would be nice, Matilda!"

"Th-this is...as fast as I can go...!"

The response Thea got back was hardly heartening, but as luck would have it, Matilda was actually a decent walker. Despite Thea's daily training, Matilda was actually managing to keep pace with her as she ran. However, her stamina was a different story. She started slowing down.

The men's shouting grew nearer by the moment.

"——!"

Thea felt something hit her shoulder.

Based on the impact, they must have thrown a rock at her. It hurt, but she wasn't about to let that stop her.

"Get the other one, too!"

Thea clutched her shoulder as she fled from the angry cries.

"Don't worry. I sent someone on ahead of you."

All of a sudden, Thea heard the high-pitched ringing of a bell echoing through the night.

Thea didn't hesitate. She headed straight toward it.

"An assassin so overpowered she can bury her foes with no weapon and without letting them sense a lick of hostility."

As she listened to Monika's explanation, the source of the noise came into view.

A blond girl as beautiful as a doll stood by the base of the cliffside.

"How unlucky..."

As she rang her handbell, she let out a low murmur.

"I'm code name Fool—and it's time to kill with everything."

Thea couldn't help but gawk at how impossible the sight before her was.

Monika had called the girl overpowered, and Thea had to agree. She defied all reason. In a sense, she was a better assassin than even Corpse.

Erna looked quietly up the cliff.

As she did, boulders the size of human heads started raining from the sky.

The girls rendezvoused at a park full of fountains.

Thea gave her report first: how one of their pursuers had taken a hit, how it hadn't been fatal, and how she and Matilda had been able to use that opening to hail a taxi and escape.

Then Monika filled in the other side of the story: how the noise from the falling rocks had reached the restaurant, but how it hadn't been enough to cause a panic, and how all the suspicious people had left.

After they finished exchanging information, Thea walked over to Matilda, who was hanging her head.

She cut to the chase. "Are you being followed?"

Matilda averted her eyes. "I…"

"If you don't tell us what's going on, I can't let you see Annette anymore."

It was harsh, but she had to do it. She couldn't trust Annette with someone sketchy.

Matilda bit her lip in resignation. "They were debt collectors."

"What do you mean?"

"…It all started two days ago."

Matilda went on to apologetically tell her tale.

"After I finished the job, I went to a park to rest for a bit, and before I knew it, someone stole my toolbox. I looked everywhere for it, but it turned out they'd already pawned it. That was when I panicked… I needed to buy it back, so I used my passport as collateral to borrow some money and tried to gamble my way for the rest. But I lost big…"

Monika cut in, her voice thick with exasperation. "Yeah, of course you did. Just go to the police."

Although it was true that there were plenty of casinos in the area, all of them were run by people who operated on the shady side of the law. An amateur going to one with some chump change would just end up as a feast for the wolves.

"Once you do, you'll be able to forget the stupid toolbox and go home."

Matilda clenched her fists in frustration. "But…there are really important things in there."

"Thea, I'm pulling the plug." Monika sounded completely fed up. "You think being with a mom like that's gonna make Annette happy? She couldn't hold a decent conversation with her own daughter, and she's loaded with debt. We're dropping her off at the embassy, and that'll be that."

Tears began welling up in Matilda's eyes. Perhaps she, too, was lamenting how poorly her conversation with Annette had gone. It was heartrending.

"Hey, keep your voice down. Matilda was the victim here, you know."

"And?" Monika shrugged. She didn't look the slightest bit fazed.

Suddenly, they heard a confident voice. "That girl is an angel."

At first, they didn't even realize it was Matilda's. Unlike her usual lifeless speech, her voice now rang with will and drive.

Monika scoffed. "Say what?"

Matilda's shoulders quivered. "When I was fleeing from those debt collectors and about to fall into despair, she appeared before me... like a glittering angel... I thought my daughter was dead, but I was reunited with her. What could you call that other than a miracle...? I was nervous up until now, but I truly do love her."

She bowed so low her waist seemed liable to snap.

"All I want is to live with my daughter again. Please, let me have this second chance..."

Thea's breath caught in her throat.

The woman before them was bowing to a group of girls over a decade her juniors.

Monika, ever the stubborn one, replied in a voice dripping with contempt. "You still haven't given us a good excuse for why you can't go to the embassy or the cops..."

After sinking into contemplative silence for a moment, though, she relaxed her tense shoulders. Something had just clicked for her.

"...But I can tell you've got your reasons." She shifted her gaze.

"Annette, why don't you make the call? What do you really think of Matilda?"

Everyone turned to look at Annette, who'd been wordlessly watching the whole scene play out.

"..."

The ensuing silence seemed to last an eternity.

Eventually, though, Annette spoke. "I've seen it before."

Thea tilted her head. "Annette?"

"That toolbox... It's cobalt blue, like the color of the sky..."

Matilda covered her mouth with her hands.

Annette gazed vacantly at the sky. Her eyes were so out of focus it was like she was trying to stare at the whole of the atmosphere hanging above them.

"Someone used to carry it around so proudly..."

"Wait, are your memories—?"

"But back then, it was so big, and so heavy, and so hard, and so close, and it hurt…"

She trailed off.

Her shoulders slumped, and she let out a long exhale. A cheerful smile spread across her face. "Nope! I can't remember anything, yo."

And with that, Annette had nothing left to say, apparently.

Was she starting to change?

Thea got a vague feeling she was.

Had something taken root in that emptiness she'd sensed in Annette? Had meeting Matilda triggered that?

That was something to be celebrated. She couldn't afford to let this opportunity pass them by.

"Here's a question for you, Matilda." Thea laid her hand atop her chest. "Would you mind if I went and retrieved your toolbox for you?"

Matilda stared at her in complete astonishment.

◇◇◇

Later that night, Thea quietly slipped out of their hotel dressed in her mission gear. The black of her outfit melted into the night, all but erasing her from sight. She slunk through darkened alleyways to avoid drawing attention.

Even at night, the city's lights burned bright.

Tourists strutted their way down the main drag in hopes of checking out the fountains and catching the light shows. Thea saw them and anxiously quickened her pace. The Din Republic was a relatively safe place, but even it had its share of gangs and other criminals—especially in a city as full of easy marks as this one.

A twinge ran through her shoulder.

She had her earlier rock injury to thank for that, no doubt. She was just lucky it had been a rock and not a bullet.

Thea didn't know what kind of group it was that had ripped Matilda off. If things turned violent, there was a fair chance she wouldn't get off so easy a second time.

However, she was the one who had decided to go in alone. She didn't want to get the others caught up in all this.

Right as she thought back to that decision, a familiar figure stood blocking her way.

It was Monika.

"What? Are you here to stop me?"

"Are you serious about all this?" Monika asked. She, too, was wearing her mission gear. "Why go out of your way to help her? There's no way it's worth the risk."

"I told you, didn't I? Annette's heart is empty. I want to help her."

"And what if doing that makes her want to stop being a spy?"

"Then Annette"—Thea gave her a small smile—"can go back to being a normal teenage girl."

"………"

"Monika?"

Monika raised her hand to her mouth and sank into thought. On second glance, Thea noticed the mirror she was holding. It looked like she was checking her backside.

"There's a big army presence here," Monika murmured quietly. "It's been bothering me for a while. Ever since this afternoon, there've been a bunch of soldiers milling about. Too many."

"But why?"

"Probably 'cause of some sort of mess that's going on. A mess that we don't want to get involved in."

Ever since the end of the war, the bulk of the army's duties had been in border control, disaster relief, training, and helping out the police when things got too big for them to handle—namely, in situations involving terrorists and spies.

Thea, too, had gotten the feeling that something was off. However…

"You sure you don't want to back out?"

Thea nodded. "Certain."

"You really are an idiot. And after you took that hit earlier, too."

Monika sounded exasperated, but she was smirking as she pointed at Thea's shoulder.

"Wouldn't have happened if we'd taken another approach, you know. If I'd taken Matilda, and you'd handled comms, we could've gotten out of there without screwing up like that."

"Maybe, but I'm the one who got us into this. I can't have other people taking on all the danger for me."

Thea had noticed Monika's disapproval when she'd given the order earlier.

She also knew full well that Monika could have gotten rid of the hoodlums on her own.

"It's the same deal this time around. I'm the one who offered to help, so I have to take responsibility for my decision."

"…There you go again with the idiocy."

"Wha—?"

When Thea tried to demonstrate her resolve, Monika shot her right down. She seemed even more exasperated than before.

"When you get hurt, it makes *me* look like I'm not doing *my* job."

"But that's just not true. And if anyone thinks that, I'll be sure to explain what really—"

"Our teammates might not see it that way. In the end, I'm gonna take the heat for letting you make such dumb choices."

"Ah—"

Thea couldn't come up with a rebuttal. That possibility had completely slipped her mind.

"I—I am sorry about that, but I can't just leave Matilda to—"

"That's why I'm here to help." Monika gave Thea a soft clap on the arm.

Thea stared at her in shock.

"You're really…"

"Geez, just take a hint. Look, you know how I am about pride. If one of my teammates gets hurt, it reflects badly on me. If you're not gonna back down, what choice do I have?" Monika let out a protracted sigh. "Just this once, I'll be one of your good little girls."

When she did, another pair of people popped out of the shadows.

"I'm coming, too."

"Me too, yo."

It was Erna and Annette, both clad in their mission gear.

"………"

Thea's lips trembled.

Her body suddenly felt hot all over. She unconsciously took in a big breath and filled her lungs to the brim.

Monika raised an eyebrow in distaste. "What?"

"I just can't believe it. I was so sure you were coming here to shout at me. 'Get your ass back in line, slut.'"

"You don't think very highly of me, do you?"

"And also…I feel so encouraged."

At long last, the four of them were finally working together.

Unable to stop a smile from spreading across her face, Thea combed back her hair. "Now, let's do this! With the four of us together, there's nothing we can't—"

"Yeah, no." Monika shut her rousing speech down cold. "We're not those four from the unchosen squad, so we don't need to pretend to be all buddy-buddy."

After ungraciously referring to Lily, Grete, Sybilla, and Sara as the unchosen squad, Monika rolled her shoulders. It was pompous as hell, but that was Monika for you.

"We're gonna cooperate our way, and we're gonna do it with the pride of knowing we were the chosen ones."

There seemed to be no end to her arrogance.

However, it would be a lie to say that her words didn't fill Thea's heart with excitement.

The first ones into the fray were Thea and Erna.

They found the store they were looking for directly off the road leading to the station and managed to slip inside right before closing. The store was cramped and filled with glass showcases featuring everything from gemstones to brand-name leather accessories.

The lighting in here is so poor… It's like they aren't interested in actually selling anything.

Spies had keen intuitions for those sorts of discrepancies.

Annette had scoped out the pawnshop ahead of time, and when Thea and Erna went to a specific shelf, they found a cobalt-blue toolbox sitting there just like she said they would. It was placed in a conspicuous spot visible even from outside.

Thea looked at the price tag, then did a double take. That was almost twice what the average adult man made in a month.

Something is definitely up. No normal toolbox would command a price like that.

Matilda had given up on buying it straight up and gone to the casino to try to earn more, and with a price like that, Thea could understand why.

She was starting to see the malicious trap Matilda had gotten caught in.

"Excuse me, but I have something I'd like to sell. Do you have a moment?"

The shopkeeper, a gaunt young man wearing glasses, was in the back.

He looked harmless enough at first glance, but he had the hungry, overpowering eyes of a predator.

"Would you be willing to buy this from me?" Thea took out a different toolbox and offered it to the man.

It was a perfect replica of the one Matilda had stolen from her.

"I can give you..." The man scribbled his fountain pen across a piece of paper as he stared drearily at her. "...this much."

His offer was mind-bogglingly paltry.

"Oh dear." Thea's eyes went wide with surprise the very way a naive, sheltered young lady's would. "But it's exactly the same as that one over in the showcase, isn't it? Can't you give me at least seventy percent of the selling price?"

From the outside, Thea's toolbox looked like a perfect copy of Matilda's stolen one.

Not only had Annette whipped it up, she had done so in less than an hour. A single glance at the one in the showcase had been enough for her to memorize its appearance, and from there, she'd modified a store-bought toolbox until it looked identical.

The shopkeeper raised his glasses in shock.

"*E-exactly* the same?"

He couldn't believe his eyes. That was just how elaborate Annette's counterfeit was.

The two boxes were identical, inside and out. There was no good excuse he could give to justify valuing them differently.

Thea gave him a smile as sweet as sugar and lightly placed her hand on Erna's back.

"Please, sir. It was very precious to her father, you know."

"Look, I'd love to help you, but my hands are tied."

"Isn't there anything you can do? If we don't get that money soon..."

Thea clutched the shopkeeper's hands and looked deep into his eyes. His face went flush as he stared back at her.

She held his gaze for exactly three seconds. That was all she needed.

"…I'm sorry for asking so much of you." She let go of his hands and gave him a delicate smile. "This is the hotel we're staying at. If you change your mind, please don't hesitate to call."

She pressed the note into the shopkeeper's hand and left the store alongside Erna. As they left, she made sure to brush Erna's hair back over her ear, just in case. Her luscious blond locks gleamed as they caught the light.

The shopkeeper was sure to remember that hair, if nothing else.

Once they were out, Thea spoke into her transceiver.

"This is Dreamspeaker. Stage one is complete. I saw right through the shopkeeper's desires—he's a money-grubber, that's for dang sure. Our suspicions were right on the money."

She knew exactly what the man was going to do next.

"I'm sending Fool to walk to the false hotel site. This part might take a while, so just hold your position."

As Monika held her position in the back alley, her transceiver buzzed a second time.

"*This is Fool. Stage two is finished.*"

Barely any time had passed since Thea had called in. This time, the voice on the other end was Erna's.

"*They stole the toolbox, just like we planned.*"

That was fast. Things were moving along swifter than they'd expected.

"Good, that means we were right about the pawnshop and the thieves working together."

Delighted that he'd found an easy mark, the man from the pawnshop must have gotten in touch with his buddies and told them to lie in wait on the path between the pawnshop and the hotel Thea mentioned so they could steal a toolbox from a girl with blond hair. There was no way it was all a coincidence.

"…Still, that was weirdly fast."

"*They got away while I was distracted by a water show.*"

"You're like a pickpocket's wet dream."

"*That reminds me, I haven't seen my purse in a few—*"

Monika stowed her transceiver in her pocket. It sounded like Erna had run into some trouble of her own, but Monika decided to leave that for Thea to deal with.

"Annette, what's the status on the homing device?"

"Working like a charm, yo. And it's pretty close."

Annette danced around holding a locator. They had placed its homing device inside Annette's counterfeit toolbox.

She followed the beacon and led Monika to a small building sandwiched between a pair of mega-hotels. A group of suit-wearing men with wicked smiles on their faces milled about the seedy-looking office in the building's semibasement.

"These punks aren't even a proper gang. Where's the fun in that?" Monika slumped her shoulders as she peeked in through the window. "Well, whatever. Let's get this over with."

She pulled a mask down over her face, kicked in the window, and leaped through it.

Inside, a woman let out a scream. "Wh-who are you?!"

"Just a tourist passing through."

As Monika gave her a listless reply, she looked around the room.

There were five people in the semibasement room: one woman and four men. A stack of backpacks and other stolen goods sat piled around the room, and over in the back, she saw a safe. It had a cylinder lock rather than a combination lock, and it was dirt cheap. Monika could have it open in seconds.

Annette's counterfeit toolbox sat right beside it.

"This is a pretty messed-up operation you've got going on. You steal valuables from tourists, sell 'em to that pawnshop, and then what? You have the pawnshop put the goods up for exorbitant prices, then lend money to the marks and lead them to your casino? Not bad, not bad. Been a while since I ran into any scumbags that thorough." Monika started riffling through the items strewn haphazardly across the room's table. "Lotta collateral passports you've got, huh?"

She flipped through the passports, checking each one's contents as she went.

Upon finding the one she was looking for, she chuckled. "...Yeah, that's what I figured."

One of the men shouted in anger. "Hands off the merch!"

He grabbed a lead pipe lying nearby and charged at Monika.

She deftly sidestepped the attack, and when he came back for round two, she swept his legs out from under him. His momentum sent him crashing right into the safe, where he hit his head and fell unconscious.

That was enough for the others to realize that there was more to their intruder than met the eye. They drew their knives and moved to surround her.

However, it would take a lot more than that to shake Monika.

"Look, I'd be happy to take you all down myself…but this time, I'm handing off the honors," she said, sounding almost bored. She snapped her fingers.

"Yo, is this where I come in?"

Annette poked her head in through the broken window. Her pure-hearted smile seemed wildly out of place in a situation as tense as the one going on inside.

As the men stared at her in shocked disbelief, Monika pulled a pair of goggles out of her pocket.

The men had no way of knowing what was about to happen.

The toolbox may have looked perfectly innocent, but the moment they carelessly accepted one of Annette's inventions into their hideout was the moment they sealed their own defeats.

"I'm code name Forgetter—and it's time to put it all together, yo."

Tear gas began billowing from the toolbox.

The meeting spot was a grassy park.

When they showed up the next afternoon with the toolbox, Matilda's eyes went wide.

"…How did you get it back? Who exactly are you all?"

Thea dodged the question with a quick lie. "One of my relatives is a cop. I just called them up and asked them to do me a favor."

The truth was that Monika had stolen the thieves' ledger from the tear gas–filled room and used it to blackmail the pawnshop owner into giving back the toolbox. They would have liked to get Matilda's passport back as well, but Monika had said she couldn't find it in the room.

However, telling Matilda what had actually gone down wasn't on their agenda for the day.

Beside them, Annette was hyperventilating.

"Hey, let's focus!" She hopped up and down. "I wanna see what's inside there, yo!"

"Of course, if you want..."

"I was so excited for this, I couldn't sleep last night!" Annette tugged on Matilda's shirt and forced her to take a seat atop the lawn. "I wanna make it so that only my targets fall for my traps. The other day, I set a trap for Bro, but then Erna fell for it like a big old klutz. What should I do?"

"Hmm? You mean, for pranks? Um... What about using this paint, then?"

"What's it do, what's it do?"

"It's a new water-soluble paint we just developed. It dissolves in water, so you can use it to differentiate real things and their copies. You could try only teaching the trick to your friends, maybe?"

"Ooh! I'm blown away, yo!"

By the look of it, Matilda's toolbox was full of the materials she was researching. The pawnshop owner hadn't been able to sell them because he hadn't known what he was looking at.

Mother and daughter sat together in the park under the afternoon sun and exchanged a lively conversation with an array of machine parts and blueprints spread out before them.

It made for a rather odd sight, but the two of them seemed to be enjoying themselves.

"Wow! Now I want this toolbox and everything in it, yo!"

"I—I'm sorry, but you can't have it. I need it for my work."

Whenever Annette dragged the conversation in a new direction, Matilda would be left hurriedly having to catch up.

Unlike at the restaurant, though, both of them were being perfectly eloquent.

"You know, I bet that's what their conversations were like before, too," Thea remarked.

"Yeah," Erna agreed.

The two of them nodded in perfect sync as they watched Annette and Matilda from a distance.

Annette's expression was like that of a child who'd just found a wonderful new toy. In all their time together at Lamplight, Thea had never seen her like that before. That interaction right there was moving Annette's heart more than a thousand fancy dinners ever could have.

Thea felt a profound sense of accomplishment, but at the same time, she got a twinge in her heart.

What if Annette really does decide she wants to go live with Matilda?

It was gauche of her to be regretful after coming this far. She knew that.

But at the same time, she couldn't help but feel conflicted.

Beside her, Erna spoke quietly. "...There's something I want to say for the record." She stuffed one of the donuts she was snacking on into her mouth and frowned. "I hate her."

"What?"

"I hate Annette."

"B-but why?" Thea responded to the sudden confession with shock, and Erna stamped her feet.

"Because she always bullies me, that's why!"

"Oh. Right."

Out of all the girls, Erna was the one who most often found herself on the receiving end of Annette's mayhem. If it wasn't a squirt gun attack, it was a nighttime kick to the face, and if it wasn't that, it was something else.

Erna's voice grew quieter. "...But I'll still miss her if she leaves."

In a way, it sounded like she was indirectly blaming Thea. To her, it probably looked like Thea was trying to drive Annette away from the group.

"Please, Erna, don't get me wrong." Thea stroked Erna's head. "I don't think Matilda would make a very good mother at all. She doesn't seem one bit reliable, and if Annette says she wants to go live with her, I'm going to do my best to try to talk her out of it."

"Huh?"

"But if that's what Annette really wants, then she'll have my blessing."

The most important thing was what Annette wanted.

All Thea was doing was laying out her options to try to foster her emotional growth. She didn't *want* Annette to go live with Matilda. Far from it.

Her hope was that Annette would choose Lamplight of her own free will. That was the only stake she had in this.

"I think that's very noble of you, Big Sis Thea."

"Why, thank you."

Hearing her teammate's praise filled Thea with satisfaction all over again.

Her heart was full of thoughts of the spy she was trying to emulate.

Surely, the hero she so admired would have made the same decision she had.

Annette continued peppering her mother with questions until well into the evening.

By the end of it, Matilda looked bone-tired. By the time Annette finally chirped "I learned a lot, yo!" and released her, she looked to be on the verge of passing out.

Matilda staggered unsteadily over to Thea—

"She's incredible… It took us years to develop those materials and devices, and she was able to understand how they worked like it was nothing…"

—and let out a sigh of amazement.

There was a hint of pride lurking in her expression. Spending time with her daughter like that must have been just as fulfilling as it looked.

Thea promised to get in touch soon, and the two parties went their separate ways. The next time they met, they would need to make sure to consult with Klaus first and make a final decision.

As they headed back to the hotel, Annette murmured in a voice that sounded rather moved. "So *that's* what a mom is." It would seem that the daughter had gotten a lot out of the exchange, too.

Annette was all smiles the entire way back to the hotel. When they returned to their room, Monika greeted them with a book in one hand.

"Heya."

She had insisted she had something she needed to do alone, so she had spent the day separate from Thea and the others. Thea had given her the go-ahead. She knew how loath Monika was to work with others, and she was impressed she'd put up with it for so long.

That was right—today was the last full day of their vacation.

Tomorrow night, they would have to head back to Heat Haze Palace. Realizing that made Thea feel a touch of melancholy.

"Likewise to you," Thea replied. "Matilda was thrilled, and it was all thanks to you."

"Nah, I barely did anything. If anyone should take the credit, it's Annette."

"Heh. I told you, didn't I? Together, we're unbeatable."

"And *I* told *you*, I'm plenty unbeatable on my— Ah, forget it. It's exhausting, constantly having to make comebacks."

Monika gave a vaguely vexed wave. She was being her usual blunt self, but her heart wasn't really in it.

"You know, Monika, our vacation's over tomorrow. What say we spend tonight cutting loose? We can all hit the town together," Thea suggested.

She and Monika had been fighting like cats and dogs throughout the entire trip, but she felt like this was her chance to finally deepen their bond. It would be nice to spend time with her outside of a mission for once.

"Feels like if I hang out with you, it'll put my wallet in danger," Monika retorted. "But I guess just this once can't hurt."

"Then, it's decided. Come on, everyone, to the casino!"

"Hold up," Monika replied. "You and I are one thing, but it'll look like we have two kids in tow. They'll kick us out in a heartbeat."

Erna raised her hand. "...I've always wondered what casinos are like. I want to go!"

Monika threw a pillow at Erna to make her be quiet. "You, of all people, are not allowed to gamble." Then she gave them all a cheery smile. "But hey, we can worry about all that once we're off the clock."

"What do you mean?" Thea asked.

"We gotta report in to Klaus. About Matilda."

"Ah, right..."

What would Klaus decide to do?

They had spent nearly three months with the man, but none of them could claim to understand him in any real capacity.

"I wonder what Teach will say... Honestly, I'm a little bit scared to find out. Maybe he'll say I was wrong to even let Annette and Matilda meet in the first place."

Their suite was equipped with a direct-dial phone. If they put in their special number and gave the right password to the operator, they could connect directly to Heat Haze Palace.

Thea's expression darkened as she looked at the phone.

Monika laughed. "Well, the good news is you don't have to worry about that anymore."

"What do you mean?"

"What I mean is: The situation is bigger than that."

Thea didn't follow.

Beside her, Erna gave Monika a quizzical look, and Annette wore an innocent smile.

With all eyes on her, Monika began explaining herself with great amusement.

"None of it added up. She hesitated before giving out the name of her hotel, she got mugged and wouldn't go to the cops... A little digging, and there it was. I found a passport with Matilda's photo in it, but a totally different name. And I bet that's why there was such a big military presence here, too."

Apparently, Monika *had* found Matilda's passport.

Why had she hidden that from them? And what was it she'd spent the entire day investigating?

"What are you saying...?"

"I'm saying thanks. Thanks to you guys, I was able to crack the case."

As Thea looked at her, flustered, Monika delivered her conclusion.

"Matilda is an Imperial spy."

And that was that.

Upon seeing Monika's triumphant smile, Thea finally realized what she'd been up to.

That was why she'd been so oddly cooperative.

She had seen this development coming, and she'd used Thea and the others to achieve her own ends. That team unity she'd displayed? All an act.

"Here, let me go ahead and report in to Klaus." Monika walked over to the phone and began spinning the dial. "After all, it's our job to hand her over to the military, right?"

Her smile was as cruel as the reaper's.

Interlude
Missing ③

It was right around noon when the train reached their stop.

The moment they stepped off the platform, Lily let out a coo of amazement.

"Wh-whoa, this place is nicer than the capital!"

Even a single glance was enough to spot over a dozen of the massive, ritzy hotels that stood towering around the station. Lily felt like she was standing in the middle of the massive citadel. It was said that most of the tourists who visited there were so awed they had trouble so much as putting one foot in front of the other, and Lily was no exception.

She was born in the sticks and had grown up living in a spy academy dorm, and by the look of it, she wasn't quite used to big cities. Her reaction was a bit odd, given that she'd recently been to the Imperial capital, which was miles more advanced, but it was what it was.

"Just in the areas around the hotels." After replying, Klaus lowered his voice. "More importantly, how many do you see?"

The station building had two stories, and throngs of people were milling about both of them. Just past the ticket gates, there were a variety of stalls selling everything from maps to soft drinks, and out front, people waiting for rides to their hotels were lined up at the pickup-drop-off area.

However, not everyone present was there for happy reasons. One group in particular practically radiated tension.

"I count...twelve soldiers?"

There was a group clad in full military uniforms shooting pointed looks at people as they passed through the ticket gates.

Lily blinked. "No, there's another seven mixed in with the crowd and wearing plain clothes. I think they're trying to be covert, but between their physiques and how menacing they look, they stick out like sore thumbs."

"That's the armed forces for you."

When it came to espionage work, they were worse than useless. Such was the difference between the hand-selected, hand-trained members of the Foreign Intelligence Office and the army, that would take any young adult with a pulse.

"Still, remember that the army's power lies in its numbers. They may be weak individually, but they have enough manpower to allot nine-teen soldiers just to cover the station."

Being able to throw that many bodies at an enemy spy was a strength in and of itself.

With his voice still low, Klaus posed a question to Lily.

"If it was up to you, how would you break through their siege? Assume that they know what you look like."

"Wait, a pop quiz?"

Lily rubbed her chin and hmmed thoughtfully.

"W-well, I'd start by using poison to knock out whoever looked like they were the most important person—"

"If you did that, you would die like a balloon fluttering through the air."

"I don't quite follow, but...you're saying I lost?"

Upon seeing how the soldiers had been stationed, Klaus could tell that they had a skilled commanding officer calling the shots. Further-more, he had a pretty good idea who that might be.

Klaus headed toward the hotel he'd been told about in advance. The army had rented out a large room in a first-class hotel to use as their command-and-control center.

En route, he stopped in an alley and instructed Lily to hide her face under a hood.

"What, I can't let them see my face?"

"The army is a leaky ship. If our soldiers get a good look at your face, you should assume that it won't be long before that intel makes its way

into enemy hands. All my information's already been leaked, but you need to be careful about who sees you."

"...Teach, you seem tense."

"There's a man in the army I don't get along with."

When the two of them reached the sixth floor, they ran into a soldier blocking the hallway. Klaus's declaration that they were with the Foreign Intelligence Office earned them a glower, but the soldier stood aside all the same.

Inside the command-and-control center, seven men were sitting around a large table with a map spread out atop it. They all had their arms crossed, and when they realized Klaus had rudely come in without so much as knocking, they collectively gasped.

The young man sitting in the middle stood up and walked over to Klaus with wide strides.

"Hey, what the hell are you doing here?! If I went asking the Foreign Intelligence Office for help, I think I'd remember it."

It was obvious from his outfit that he was a military man, and between his short, evenly trimmed blond hair and his muscular physique, he cut an imposing form. He looked to be about twenty-four, but his face did not convey the inexperience you would expect for a man that young.

He was the aforementioned man Klaus didn't get along with— Captain Welter Barth.

"I'm under no obligation to answer that question. We have a right to operational secrecy." Klaus exhaled, then went on. "Now, tell me everything the military knows about the situation."

"Is that any way to ask someone for a favor?" Welter scowled at him. "The local police and my men worked their asses off gathering this intel, and you—"

"Enough with the posturing. You know the rules."

"You're a real piece of work, you know that?"

"Also, you don't have to get right up in my face. It's hot in here."

Welter glared at Klaus like it was taking everything he had not to grab him by the collar right then and there.

Klaus, who appeared to have no interest in playing nice, merely ignored him.

Lily could tell how tense the situation was. She decided to step in. "Um, do you two know each other?"

That was when Welter noticed her for the first time. His expression softened. "Well, that's new. It's not every day you show up with a sub-ordinate in tow."

Lily gave him a nervous bow. "Flower Garden, Foreign Intelligence Office."

Welter seemed to like that. "Welter Barth, Military Intelligence Department captain. It's a pleasure."

He shook hands with Lily, then turned back to Klaus and scowled again. "To answer your question, Bonfire and I have an interesting relationship. We've crossed paths a couple times."

"Much as I try to avoid it," Klaus shot back.

Apparently, he and Welter had known each other since Klaus's time on Inferno.

Whenever Klaus was tasked with getting intel from the military for domestic missions, he would find himself dealing with Welter surprisingly often. The man had an odd knack for sniffing out trouble. Welter was a mere warrant officer when they first met, but he rose through the ranks at a blistering clip, eventually getting promoted to captain at a rare young age.

Klaus respected the man's skills, but perhaps due to the organizations they worked for, the two of them never really saw eye to eye.

"Your superiors dragged their feet getting us the intel again. Next time, I want you to report any new developments yourself."

"Here in the army, we have something called a chain of command. You think I'm going to act without orders, just because *you* told me to?" Welter scoffed contemptuously at Klaus's complaint. "Plus, I'm no big fan of taking the information we put our lives on the line to assemble and handing it over so you can take all the credit."

"If that's what you're worried about, you need to get your priorities straight."

"If it was just my feelings at stake, I could put up with it. But this kind of stuff affects morale on the ground. People don't operate on logic alone, Bonfire. And besides, you came storming in here begging for a sitrep, but when's the last time your side ever threw us so much as a breadcrumb of intel?"

"The matters we deal with at the Foreign Intelligence Office are top secret. We can't just go handing out classified information whenever it suits your fancy."

Klaus and Welter glared at each other.

Lily started getting worried again, but this level of bickering was pretty standard for the two of them.

The fact of the matter was that the Foreign Intelligence Office did have the right to look over the military's intel.

With visible displeasure, Welter handed over a dossier.

Inside, there were pictures of the battle between the Lylat Kingdom and Galgad Empire spies, a photo of the Lylat spy's corpse, and finally, a copy of the passport belonging to the woman they suspected of being the Imperial spy.

"That woman's our spy at-large. We've got the highway, the trains, and the port locked down so tight not even a rat could get through. We've frozen her bank account, too, so it's only a matter of time before she cracks and we find her."

"That all sounds excessive. I could find her within a day."

"And how exactly would you do that? She was good enough to take out one spy already."

"I would gently scoop her up like a waterweed floating on the—"

"I don't have time for your empty bravado. Just leave her to us, okay? The brass has already—"

"It's not empty," Klaus murmured, but Welter paid him no heed.

"I'm telling you this for your own good." Suddenly, Welter lowered his voice. He didn't want any of his army colleagues to hear what he was going to say next. "I don't have to tell you how much the army hates the Foreign Intelligence Office. The brass would do anything to turn up some sort of scandal on you guys, and that goes double for these past few months."

That was no wonder—not after the egg they put on the military's face by unveiling the way they'd let their bioweapon fall into enemy hands.

Now the army was after petty revenge.

"If you go out there and end up letting the spy get away right when we have her where we want her, the brass'll be all too happy to go to Parliament and demand the Foreign Intelligence Office get disbanded."

"………"

"Look, just stand down. I might not be your biggest fan, but not even I want to see the Foreign Intelligence Office get torn down."

Welter was well aware of who Inferno was.

After hearing of their valor and skill, there were few if any who could hold any real animosity toward the Foreign Intelligence Office.

"You know what? You're right. I will head back. Thank you for the warning," Klaus said.

"See, that wasn't so hard."

"One piece of advice, though. You need more people watching the port."

Welter looked at him in confusion. "What do you mean?"

"There's no guarantee this spy is working alone. The way I see it, you haven't been watching the people coming in closely enough. If the situation drags on, we run the risk of having villains from the Empire come over to back them up."

"Spy reinforcements, huh?" Welter nodded. "That's a fair point. What makes you think it's the port we should be worried about, though?"

"I just do."

Klaus's reply earned him a frown of deep displeasure.

When they left the hotel, Lily let out a big sigh. "Well, I totally get why we and the army don't get along now."

She hid out in the back alley as she took off her cloak. Her expression was half exasperation, half resignation. She stared up at the building they'd just come out of.

"Everyone in that room up there was staring daggers at us the whole time. I mean, they hate our *guts*."

"It's been like that for a long, long time."

"I mean, yeesh. That was like the way Monika glares at me when I screw up during missions."

That second one probably wasn't hatred, but it was at least disdain.

"Still, Welter seemed like an all right guy."

"I don't care for him personally, but that isn't to say he's a bad leader. The soldiers back at the station looked like they'd been well trained," Klaus said, nodding. "Personally, though, I don't care for him."

"You really needed to say that twice?"

"He thinks everything between the two of us is a competition. It's obnoxious."

"Still, you didn't have to be that mean to him. I mean, what, do you hate him just 'cause he's in the army?"

"I hate him because he's a pompous ass."

"........................."

"Sorry, what was that? Did you say something?"

"Who, little old me?"

Klaus wasn't sure, but he felt like he'd just heard someone murmur, "You sounded pretty pompous yourself back there, Teach."

There was more he would have liked to explain, but now was hardly the time to do it.

They needed to get back to the topic at hand—the shocking truth that Welter had revealed to them.

"Anyways, about the spy the military is tracking—"

"Oh, yeah," Lily replied. "Did you figure something out?"

"That passport photo bore something of a resemblance to Annette. There might be some sort of connection there."

The forged passport had had a black-and-white photo attached to it. The name and date of birth were doubtless fake, but the spy would have had to pass through customs, so the photo was probably of her actual face.

It was a face that resembled someone they both knew well.

"Wh—?" Lily gulped. "Wait, hold on a minute! But he just said—"

Klaus nodded. He thought back to the declaration Welter had so proudly made.

"The brass has already...authorized that she be shot on sight."

If their teammates' disappearance had anything to do with that woman, then things were in danger of getting ugly.

Chapter 4

Schism

Thea thought back.

She reflected on their fight with Corpse—and how during it, the girls' sole job had been to run away.

They expected Corpse to surface so he could assassinate a major politician, and the girls' job was to find him and immediately use their radios to report his location to Klaus. Their orders were to simply observe until Klaus showed up, and if Corpse spotted them, to get away from him. That said, they couldn't afford to flee the scene entirely. If they did that, Corpse would go to ground and massacre innocent civilians to cover his tracks.

They wouldn't be fighting Corpse directly, but it was still a dangerous job.

The first one to make contact was Thea.

They were at a popular summer getaway filled with gorgeous villas, and it was there that she spotted Corpse through her binoculars.

Teach's guess was right on the money. Sure enough, here he is.

Corpse's target must have been a politician at their vacation home.

Impatience and excitement welled up within her. She'd really done it. She was the one who'd found Corpse.

A moment later, though, that feeling of pride was the furthest thing from her mind.

Corpse turned her way.

Her heartbeat quickened.

It can't be... There's almost seven hundred feet between us!

She had gotten sloppy. She knew that Klaus could have spotted her from that distance, but that fact had completely slipped her mind.

Corpse dashed straight toward her. There were all manners of villas and roadside trees blocking his way, but any hope Thea had that they might buy her some time was quickly dashed. He merely used them as footholds to accelerate faster.

He wants to catch me so he can make me talk.

Thea started running.

Her mind raced with the information on her friends' prep work that she'd drilled into her memory. Erna had told her about a series of unstable cliffs and easy-to-knock-over walls, and Annette had told her the locations of the myriad traps she'd set.

However, Corpse was no slouch. He avoided all of Erna's pitfalls and Annette's bombs like it was nothing.

"So weak."

He caught up with Thea in what felt like no time at all, and the two of them squared off.

The man really was as gaunt as his namesake. His cheekbones barely had any meat on them, and his eye sockets protruded from his face like embossed carvings. Thoughts of death flashed through her mind at his sickly appearance, and a shudder ran through her body.

She unconsciously took a step back.

"You're trying to back down? Now?" Corpse snickered. "Pathetic."

Thea bit her lip.

He was right. Due to the brick walls surrounding the villa, retreat had never been an option.

"Ugh, what a bore. Why does no one ever give me a decent fight? There's no sport in killing people like you." Corpse readied his knife and approached her.

There was no way Thea could use her ability on him in a situation like this, and Erna's and Annette's powers had been rendered useless as well.

She tried to ready her gun, but her knees were shaking so badly she couldn't get a bead on him.

There was only one girl who even stood a chance against him.

"Yikes. Nice face you got there."

Monika popped up atop the villa roof with a pithy quip and immediately opened fire.

Corpse leaped to the side on reflex and turned toward Monika, but then something unbelievable happened.

The shots ricocheted.

When Monika's bullets hit the brick outer wall, they bounced back and flew at Corpse from behind. Making them do that would have been a superhuman feat all on its own, but on top of that, she'd also made sure to draw his attention away from them with her insult.

"Now, you—you I like."

However, all the shots did was graze his shoulder. Somehow, Corpse had sensed the ricochets coming.

Thea could tell that both Monika, who had attacked her opponent by reflecting her shots, and Corpse, who had managed to dodge them anyway, were far out of her league.

Monika rubbed the back of her neck. "Never thought I'd be getting compliments from my opponent."

"For all your skills, though…" Somehow, Corpse was holding a gun. None of them had seen him draw it. "…you're still soft."

He fired a series of ultra-rapid quick-draw shots at Monika. Not only had he taken seemingly no time at all to draw his weapon, he hadn't taken any time lining up his shots, either. His perfectly polished assassination technique didn't have a single wasted movement to it.

"Rgh!"

Monika dodged the bullets by the slimmest of margins and took cover behind the brick chimney.

"Sorry, but you're no match for me. There's only one man who can take me on, and that's Bonfire." He sounded almost depressed. "I mean, what's the point? My apprentice called me up, and the way I hear it, Bonfire's nowhere around. He's off at some Uwe Appel politician guy's mansion. Sucks to be me, I guess. Ah, I wanna die."

Corpse shook his head in disappointment. He had fallen for their misdirection hook, line and sinker.

Monika stuck her head out from behind the chimney with a provocative grin. "Well, well, well. Sounds like Grete's holding up all right on her end, too."

"Huh?"

Monika raised her hand and pointed at the sky. "Try looking up."

Corpse turned his head upward as though irresistibly compelled. And the moment he did—

"Oh wait, I meant to the side."

—a hitherto unseen figure came barreling toward him with animalistic speed and drove their foot into his face as hard as they could.

It was Klaus.

After racing toward Corpse faster than the naked eye could track, Klaus gave him a picturesque high kick. Corpse's body flew effortlessly through the air and crashed hard into the brick wall.

"BONFIRE!" Corpse roared as he spat up blood. "I've waited years for this moment—for the man worthy of being my rival!"

Without even bothering to fix his stance, Corpse leveled his gun at Klaus. It was the same outrageously fast quick-draw technique he had used moments earlier. With barely six feet between them—practically point-blank—he fired.

A small metallic *clang* rang out.

Klaus was holding a knife. There were no injuries anywhere on him.

"What…?"

As Corpse stared in befuddlement, he ate a second kick right to the temporal region.

He crumpled to the ground, unconscious. His eyes rolled back in his head.

Thea's memories turned. Now that she thought about it, Klaus's mentor Guido had performed a similar technique where he deflected bullets with his sword. It made perfect sense that Klaus would have learned the same trick.

"Ah, so that's what I should've done…," Monika murmured. She sounded a little chagrined.

Klaus waved her down unconcernedly. "No, that was magnificent. Good job surviving."

"You sure it was the right call, taking him out that quick?" Monika asked. "Sounded like he had something he wanted to say about 'rivals' and 'fate bringing you together' or something."

"I don't recall agreeing to any of that."

Klaus looked down at Corpse in irritation. The two of them had been on different pages in that regard.

Erna and Annette stuck their heads out from behind the villa, then helped each other carry a large suitcase over.

Klaus took it, folded Corpse's body up, and stuffed it inside.

"...Aren't you going to kill him?" Thea asked.

According to the brief, their mission was to assassinate him. Did Klaus want to bring him to a secondary location first?

"Allow me to explain." Klaus slammed the suitcase shut. "Although we're given orders to kill when we're dealing with foes as dangerous as him, the best-case scenario is actually if we're able to capture them alive. The more skilled a spy, the more valuable the information they'll have is. Our job now is to hand him off to a specialist team so they can interrogate him. They'll make him take truth serum, as well as torture him if necessary."

"He's going to be tortured...?"

"Burn this memory into your mind. When an operative gets captured, all that awaits them is a darkness deeper than death."

The look in Klaus's eyes was as cold as ice. There was a hardness to his gaze that he rarely showed.

A faint chill ran across Thea's skin.

"There's no way out for them. Either their hearts give out first, and their minds shatter, or their bodies can't handle the torture, and they die. There are rare instances of people getting spared when they volunteer to serve as double agents..."

Klaus's voice deepened to emphasize his final statement.

"...but those traitors just meet death at their old comrades' hands."

Those words were no doubt meant as a warning.

He was reminding them that during their next international mission, getting captured wasn't an option.

However, none of them could have imagined that his words would end up hitting home in a completely different way so soon afterward.

"After all, it's our job to hand her over to the military, right?"

Monika's words reminded Thea of what Klaus had just taught them about what happened to captured spies. About the merciless torture that awaited them.

Her body moved on its own.

As Monika picked up the receiver, Thea ripped the phone's cord out of the wall.

"Hold on, now! Do you even realize what it is you're doing?!" Thea cried.

"You stole the words right out of my mouth. Do *you*?"

Thea and Monika glared daggers at each other as they stood in their fancy hotel room. They knew that Erna and Annette were silently watching them from the side, but they didn't exactly have the bandwidth to spare worrying about them.

Thea grabbed Monika by the collar. "You're seriously planning on turning Matilda in?!"

Monika's expression was as composed as could be. "Of course I am. She's a spy who sneaked into our borders. In case you forgot, that makes her our enemy."

"But she's Annette's *mother!*"

"And you think that pardons her crimes?" Monika spat.

She was right. The Galgad Empire had been using spies to invade their nation, and even just recently, they had sent the heartless assassin Corpse over to do his murderous work on their soil. Just like Corpse, Matilda posed a potential threat to the Republic. The four of them had a duty to neutralize her.

All that said, though…

Thea glanced back and took a look at Annette's expression. She appeared just as shocked as the rest of them. Her ever-present smile was gone, and her eyes were as wide as dinner plates.

"Look, we were always gonna have to tell Annette sooner or later." Monika, having sensed what Thea was thinking, let out a laugh. "If you wanna shout at me for how I did it, you're barking up the wrong tree."

She stooped down to escape Thea's grasp, then swept Thea's legs out from under her. Thea crumpled to the ground without even getting a chance to catch herself.

"Get your act together." Monika straightened her collar back out. "Look, all I'm doing is discussing the situation with Klaus. That's what subordinates are supposed to do, right? Surely you can't fault me for that."

"But if you do that…"

That was no compromise. It was forcing the conclusion.

"And then if Teach tells you to, you're going to turn Matilda in?"

"Well, yeah. I mean, we wouldn't even have to do anything. We could just call up the army and tell them where she is."

"So you would send her mom off to get tortured to death, and you want Annette to just accept that?!"

"...Yes?"

The flippant way Monika said it caused a seething rage to boil up inside Thea.

Why did she have to be so uniquely talented at rubbing people the wrong way? There was something fundamentally messed up about her as a person.

Right as Thea was about to give in to her anger and verbally tear Monika a new one, someone else's voice cut in.

"It'll...it'll be okay, I'm sure it will!"

It was Erna.

Her eyebrows were contorted, and she looked like she was on the verge of tears.

"I'm sure Teach will be able to think up some wonderful way for us to get through this. Some way where you two don't have to fight."

"See, Erna gets it." Monika clapped her hands. "You heard her. It'll be 'wonderful.' I mean, this is Klaus we're talking about. He'll be able to come up with some perfect solution that none of us could've ever dreamed of."

"Oh, get real!" Thea bellowed, unable to hold back her anger any longer.

Erna's shoulders twitched.

"There's no proof of that, and you both know it."

What they were describing was possible, that much was true. There was a chance that Klaus would come up with an idea that would leave everyone happy. Oh, what a pleasant future that would be.

But...what if he didn't?

She remembered his eyes when he gazed down at Corpse.

Thea knew that Klaus cared about his teammates. However, she also knew that the proper thing for spies to do was mercilessly interrogate their captured foes.

Klaus might let Matilda live, but he just as easily might have her killed. There was no way of knowing which way he'd lean.

In all their time at Lamplight, they'd never had to deal with a situation this delicate before. Thea couldn't predict what Klaus would do.

That meant that relying on him wasn't an option.

"Then, what would you have us do? Just look the other way?" Monika laughed scornfully. "I mean, I guess that'd be fine. With the way things are going, I'd say there's a good chance the army finds her for us anyway."

Thea gasped.

Monika had a point. The city was practically crawling with soldiers, and they all had their eyes peeled for Matilda.

It was only a matter of time before she got taken in, and when it came to dealing with spies, there was little difference between the Foreign Intelligence Office and the army. Either one would be perfectly happy to torture Matilda to death.

"And before you go saying anything stupid, let me remind you of something," Monika continued. "If you try to help Matilda out, that'd make you a traitor to the state. And by extension, a traitor to Lamplight."

"………"

"I guess you're not my biggest priority, though."

As Thea faltered over her response, Monika turned her gaze over to the girl who'd been silent through the entire discussion.

"Annette, you get it, right?"

Hearing her name did nothing to shake the stony expressionlessness from Annette's face. "I…"

Her lips moved.

"I………"

She started to say something but trailed off. It didn't look like she was going to finish her sentence.

Thea couldn't bear to watch.

Monika was forcing her to make a terrible decision—whether she was prepared to sacrifice her own mother.

"That's enough." Thea stepped in front of Annette. "Look, we know you're right, but this? This is just cruel. You think you can pile all that on her, and she'll just nod along and give you the go-ahead?"

"Fine. For Annette's sake, you get one day."

Monika heaved a bored-sounding sigh, then began getting her things together to head out.

She was probably doing it to gather more intel. It wasn't like she had the social graces to be excusing herself out of concern for others, after all.

"But tomorrow night, I'm making that call. That's your time limit."

The following night was when they were scheduled to head back to base. That was their deadline in more ways than one.

"Thea, Annette, I'm trusting you'll make the proper decision as spies."

Monika's final words had a chill to them that ran across Thea's throat like a knife.

"Traitors or not, it'd leave a bad taste in my mouth to have to kill a teammate."

That marked a first for Thea—the first time an ally had ever threatened her life.

After Monika left the room, Thea let out a long breath. She sat down in a nearby chair and hung her head.

How did things get like this…?

As far as she could recall, all her decisions had been fine.

She'd been doing her best. She had brought Annette and her mother together out of a desire to bring Annette happiness, but it had advanced Lamplight's needs at the same time. She'd been giving it her utmost to uphold her pride as a spy and to protect the country that her idol so loved.

Her, a traitor? It didn't make a lick of sense.

And how is it that Monika always seems to get the better of me?

The frustration she felt was simple envy.

She knew it was an ugly emotion—and misdirected, to boot—but that didn't stop her from feeling it.

How was it that she worked tirelessly for the sake of the team, and yet that aloof girl was always able to find so much more success?

Thea shook her head to clear it of those useless thoughts.

"……………Annette." Even she could tell how exhausted her own voice sounded. "Everything Monika just said is true. This is your choice to make. Asking Teach what to do would be a good decision, but if we do that, there's a chance you'll never be able to see Matilda again. What is it that *you* want to do?"

The only one who could decide what would make Annette happy was Annette herself.

Thea still felt as strongly about that now as she had before.

"I…"

When Annette opened her mouth to speak, it was with none of her usual bombastic energy. And who could blame her?

"…I want to see Matilda again, yo."

Hearing her answer filled Thea with renewed conviction in the choice she'd made.

If Annette had said "I dunno" or "Either way's fine," Thea would have been crestfallen.

Now, though, she knew that something was starting to sprout in Annette's heart. Her reunion with Matilda had been a stroke of good fortune after all.

"All right. Then, tomorrow morning, I'll take you to see her."

She brushed Annette's hair and gave her a gentle smile.

At long last, Thea finally started feeling calm again.

Erna was trembling over in the corner, and Thea bowed apologetically to her. "I'm sorry for shouting earlier."

"Big Sis Thea…"

However, that wasn't what Erna was so afraid of.

She was afraid because her teary eyes had seen the future that awaited them.

"If Annette says she wants to save her mom…what are you going to do…?"

Thea went silent. She didn't have a good answer for that.

The hotel Matilda was staying at wasn't exactly the most reputable establishment around.

A little digging made it clear that its front desk didn't check their foreign visitors' passports, nor did they inquire as to the reason they were visiting. After taking payment up front, they were hands-off for the rest of the stay. It was the kind of hotel that attracted problematic patrons, and if Matilda kept staying there, it was only a matter of time until the army found her.

Monika had probably looked up the hotel as well. That must have been what had tipped her off about Matilda's secret.

Thea called Matilda at her hotel and told her to meet them at a beautiful cobblestone promenade on the coast early the next morning. Aside from passersby out jogging and such, there wouldn't be that much foot traffic at that hour.

Thea and Annette headed out a fair bit earlier than the arranged time, then used their binoculars to check out the port.

"That's a whole bunch of soldiers, yo." Annette gave the report with her usual innocent grin. A night's sleep had restored her to her normal upbeat self.

"Sure enough, they locked down the port, too…"

It seemed like a lot of effort just to catch a single person.

Was Matilda really that dangerous of a spy? Or was this just the army going overboard?

Thea was still pondering the matter when Matilda arrived.

"Ah, Thea. Good morning."

"……………Hmm?"

The moment Matilda greeted them, Annette gave her a funny look.

As Thea started wondering why, though, Annette rubbed her tummy and moaned.

"I'm starving, yo. I wanna go to a bakery now."

Apparently, she was just hungry. Thea and Matilda decided to indulge her.

Annette strode briskly atop the seaside walkway, and the other two followed after her from a few steps back.

"So today's the day you're going back to school, right?" Matilda asked. "Thank you for taking such good care of my daughter. Once I finish up my work, I'll come pay her a visit." She bowed humbly.

Thea wondered what exactly Matilda meant by "work."

Trepidation nipped at her, but she couldn't afford to back out now. She clenched her fists tight to motivate herself.

She didn't have the time left to spend beating around the bush any longer.

"I'm sorry, but I'm going to have to be blunt. Actually, I'm not sorry. You haven't been straight with us." She looked Matilda dead-on. "My friend found your passport, and the name on it wasn't Matilda."

"Wh—?"

"Tell me straight up: Are you a foreign spy?"

Matilda's face went pale. That was answer enough as she started glancing around nervously.

"Don't worry, I'm not here to turn you in." *Not yet, at least,* Thea added silently to herself. "I just need to know what it is you're actually after."

There were swarms of soldiers gathered at the station and the port, but they were absent from the seaside promenade that sat between the two.

Thea had chosen that spot so they could talk things out.

"Tell me, Matilda. Who are you, really?"

"I—I should be asking you the same thing. Who exactly are you all?"

"Stop stalling and answer the question."

"...............Your suspicions were right." Matilda let out a resigned sigh. "I work as a spy for the Galgad Empire. I didn't think my alias would work on my daughter, so I introduced myself by my real name. I actually am called Matilda, and what I told you about being separated from her four years ago was all true."

She went on to tell Thea about how she had originally worked as an Imperial engineer, but when her husband died young and she didn't have enough money to provide for her daughter, she turned to espionage to make ends meet. She was assigned to work for a foreign manufacturer and to use her position to bring cash to operatives who were on infiltration missions in foreign nations.

"Bringing a young daughter with me helped me avoid drawing suspicion, but I never thought she would end up in a train wreck while we were abroad..."

"So that was what you meant when you said you brought Annette to work with you?"

"It was. After then, when I thought she was dead, I lived like a hollow shell. I kept working as a spy because it seemed like the easiest thing to do. I suppose that's why it all went wrong." She laughed self-derisively. "I got my tools stolen, panicked, and now the army has me surrounded. What a week."

Enemies or not, that was a pretty unfortunate story.

"But, Thea, please don't get the wrong idea about me."

"And what idea would that be?"

"I admit that I lied to you about some things, but I really did mean it when I said I thought of being reunited with my daughter as a miracle. I truly do want to take her with me."

"Why, though? That daughter you loved and Annette are basically two different people." Thea deliberately posed the question to her in the cruelest way possible. "All her old memories are gone, and four long years have passed since then."

"It's not about how long it's been." A smile spread across Matilda's face. "She hasn't changed a bit. Her personality might be a little different, and she might not remember anything, but she's still my daughter." Matilda's gentle gaze rested on Annette, who was still walking ahead of them.

Annette might have heard her; her head twitched.

Matilda chuckled. "I promise: I'm going to retire as a spy the minute we get back home. We'll live peaceful lives together, and I'll never let myself get separated from her again."

Thea rubbed her fingertips together as she searched for an outlet for the emotions swirling inside her.

This was a happy ending, right? It was everything she could have dreamed of. Annette had no memories of her origin, and yet she would still get to experience a mother's love. So why did she feel so conflicted? Was it because Matilda was an enemy spy, or was it something else?

There was one question she needed answered.

"Will you? Be able to get back home, I mean."

"I…"

Matilda exhaled for so long it must have used up every last drop of air in her lungs.

"…What am I going to dooo?"

"Aren't you supposed to be a spy?"

"I'm just a lowly smuggler. I mean, I've never even killed anyone… I sent more distress calls back home than I can count, but they just ignored them… I think they're leaving me to die."

Her voice had a sort of hollow resignation to it.

"But the thing is, I can't put it off any longer. Tomorrow, I'm going for an all-or-nothing gambit. The longer I wait, the more likely the army is to find me." She clenched her fists tight. "But if there's a chance

I can live together with my daughter once this is over, it'll make it all worth it."

Thea's reply was flat and listless. "............Is that so?"

Thea declined to go into the bakery with them, insisting she didn't have much of an appetite. She sat down on a bench outside and sighed, then watched the mother-daughter pair from afar as they happily shared their bread.

At that point, she realized that her knees were shaking.

She was afraid. Afraid that what she was about to do would be a terrible mistake.

This would have all been so much easier if Matilda were a bad person. God, I'm the worst for even thinking that...

Matilda was trapped on all sides. At this rate, she really would end up getting tortured and killed.

But then, if Thea tried to help her...

...Monika will kill me...for being a traitor.

"Differences between allies are the key to a strong team."

Those had been Klaus's exact words. Or rather, they had been Hearth's, but Klaus was the one who'd repeated them.

That can't possibly be true, though. When people have wildly different values, their team just ends up crumbling.

Thea wondered what could have possibly been going through that crimson-haired spy's head when she made that statement.

If it were you, Ms. Hearth, what would you do?

Her thoughts turned.

Once again, she thought of her idol—the woman who had led Klaus as Inferno's boss.

The girl was the daughter of a well-known newspaper company's president.

Over the hundred-plus years since the Industrial Revolution, the newspaper had prospered into a major powerhouse. It was the second-oldest paper in Din, and it had a huge readership among well-educated conservatives. Left-wing groups calling for drastic reforms rose to prominence after the war, and the way the paper lambasted them played a meaningful role in driving public discourse.

That was what led to the kidnapping. At the time, the girl was eleven years old.

The newspaper had influence on par with the radio, and the girl's father held enough public trust that his stances swayed the opinions of the masses. That was more than enough reason for foreign spies to want to target the girl.

When they did, she got a taste of true despair.

The girl was held in captivity for over two weeks, and she spent the entire time being treated like an animal in a cage. After being stripped of all her possessions, she was tossed on the cold floor in nothing but her undergarments. The room smelled foul. That was due to the bucket in the corner, which was the only place she had to do her business. For the first little while, the man in charge of feeding her would run his gaze over her bare limbs with a vulgar smile, but it wasn't long before even he began averting his gaze from her and started just dumping some bread and water into her room once a day. Two weeks of not bathing made a person pretty hard on the eyes.

I want to die.

She had been born with a silver spoon in her mouth, and the suffering was too much for her to bear.

Outside her room, she could hear them speaking in a language she didn't recognize. She must have been taken all the way to another country, so she had little hope that her nation's soldiers or police would be coming for her. Her motherland's influence couldn't reach that far.

It's all over for me.

Around the time she ran out of tears to shed, she noticed someone watching her from outside the room. She could hear some sort of conversation. It sounded like a boy and a woman, but she couldn't make out what they were saying. However, it wasn't like it mattered much. She would be dead soon anyway. She simply shut her eyes.

The next moment, there was a roar so thunderous it seemed to practically turn the world on its head.

The girl was shocked.

A short while later, the door to her room swung open with a crimson-haired woman standing on the other side. Her hair was long and flowing, and between that and its vivid hue, it looked almost like her head was ablaze. It wasn't clear how old she was, but she was certainly beautiful.

"_____"

The girl stared in astonishment. Not just at the woman, but at the grisly spectacle behind her, too.

Ten bodies lay mangled on the ground.

The faces of the men who'd imprisoned her had all been crushed, obliterated by some sort of overwhelming force. The man who had looked to be their leader had a crowbar running straight through his head.

The crimson-haired woman spoke to her.

"You're little ——, right?"

Despite the ghastly scene the woman was standing amid, there wasn't so much as a drop of blood on her. The girl couldn't help but feel calmer.

She gave the woman a small nod.

"Great! Now, my friends are busy storming the bad guys' secret hideout as we speak. There was probably a mastermind who orchestrated the kidnapping, so until we find them, you'll have to stay with us."

The girl was silent.

"Can you not talk?"

She shook her head.

"Ah. Shock from the kidnapping, I'll bet."

A nod.

"Okay, try thinking of a sentence in your head. Anything is fine."

What is she talking about?

"'What is she talking about?'—that's the kind of face you're making. Did I get it?"

Huh?!

"Luckily, this isn't my first rodeo. A couple years back, a teammate of mine took in a kid who couldn't read, write, or hold a decent conversation. When we first met, I had to communicate with him by reading his expression the same way."

Oh, huh.

"Of course, I ended up spoiling him so much that he still sucks at holding conversations, but you live and learn."

What an odd woman. Despite the extreme situation they were in, just hearing her talk helped steady the girl's nerves.

"........."

The crimson-haired woman looked quizzically at the girl.

"We end up learning to read expressions as a sort of occupational hazard, but you've got some sort of special skill, too, don't you?"

Wow, she figured me out. If I look in someone's eyes, I can see into their heart a bit.

"Whoa, that's some incredible stuff."

But I don't use it much. People would think I was creepy.

"Then, do you want to look into mine?"

Can I?

"I mean, you're curious, aren't you? You want to know who it is you're dealing with."

The crimson-haired woman crouched down in front of the girl and looked her in the eye. The girl was completely filthy, but the woman didn't let that bother her.

After three seconds, it was the girl who ended up surprised.

You have a really pretty heart.

"Wow, that's so sweet of you."

What the girl had sensed in the woman was ambition of the noblest sort and a heart full of compassion for others.

Who are you? How were you able to find me?

The crimson-haired woman gave her a small smile.

"I'm a spy. And there's nowhere I wouldn't go and nothing I wouldn't do to protect you."

And that was how Hearth and the girl who would come to be called Thea first met.

From there, the girl was moved to a safe house where she spent the next ten days together with the woman.

The woman was supposedly part of a larger team, but for some reason, none of her allies ever showed themselves around the girl. The girl occasionally heard them arguing outside her room, so there were definitely at least a few of them, but none of them ever came to see her. The crimson-haired woman was the only person who ever looked after her.

Whenever the girl got bored, the woman would come and regale her with tales of spycraft.

Confidential or not, she told the girl everything—about the shadow war, about the group called Inferno, about the missions they took on, and about how quickly the silent boy they'd taken in three years earlier had grown up.

Thea often had questions, and the woman answered them all. Despite Thea not saying a word, the woman was skilled enough to be able to figure out her questions anyway.

Why do you choose to work as a spy?

The crimson-haired woman stroked her chin in thought for a moment before answering.

"*To advance war along to its next stage, I guess.*"

I don't get it.

Isn't the war over?

"*No, not by a long shot. It's impossible to free humanity from war. The destiny of all living creatures is to seek conflict. But see, for us humans, it's possible to change what war looks like.*"

How?

"*By changing the rules. War is kind of like a game, in that it has to be played in a certain way. People have been editing those rules all through-out history. That's what gave us concepts like territory and borders. That's what gave us sovereign nations. Treaties. International laws. When humankind wages its wars, it does so within those frameworks.*"

Kind of like a sport?

"*Putting it that simply might be a little disrespectful to people who've died in wars, but basically, yes. And when people get sick of fighting, they decide on new rules. The end of the Great War marked the begin-ning of wars fought with spies. Someday, war will change again, and people will fight and fight and fight and fight until they can fight no more.*"

The crimson-haired woman licked her lips.

"*But if we spies stop fighting, then we'll end up returning to that era of indiscriminate death and slaughter.*"

You mean that if you stop fighting, the Great War will start up again?

"*That's right. And it's my job to stop that from happening.*"

Wow. So you're saving the world.

"*Yep. But to tell you the truth, I didn't want to be a spy. What I really wanted to be was a hero.*"

Why's that?

"Because spies only end up saving people from their own countries. But heroes—heroes can save so much more than that."

The woman's voice sounded so proud that before the girl noticed, she was speaking, too.

Her vocal cords trembled ever so quietly. *"I want… I want to be like you, too."*

"Oh, look, you're back to talking again." Then the crimson-haired woman squinted at her. *"Wait, are you mimicking my voice?"*

It felt like I would be able to speak again if I used your voice to do it. Does this mean I'm more like you now…?

"…………"

She was worried the woman would think she was mocking her. Was she going to get mad?

The woman gave her a profound nod and patted her head.

"With your talents, you're going to end up surpassing me someday." Her words flowed eloquently. *"We don't have much more time left together, but why don't I give you some hands-on tutoring?"*

In that moment, the warmth from the woman's hand was the girl's everything.

As she sat reminiscing on the past, Thea felt a smile crawl across her face.

She seemed really nice at the time, but thinking back now, she was kind of intense, too…

Thea had grown a fair bit since then, but even now she still didn't fully understand the woman's beliefs. She had gone on and on about conflict, and even though she was full of love, she didn't hesitate to kill when she needed to. Deep in her heart, though, her sole desire was to save as many people as possible. Thea wondered how she had reconciled that contradiction.

Thinking of her always filled Thea's heart with aspiration. The way she shouldered all that responsibility, constantly pushing forward to carry out her ideals… It stirred Thea's heart.

Kindness and platitudes alone could never change the world. You needed courage, and that was something Thea knew she lacked.

"Yo, Sis."

Thea had been so lost in her memories that she barely noticed Annette standing right in front of her.

She was done chatting with Matilda, and the latter was waving good-bye to her and Thea from off in the distance. The mother-daughter bonding time had reached its conclusion.

"I got you a reward."

Annette stuffed something into Thea's mouth.

It tasted like a chocolate pastry. She must have gotten it to go from the bakery.

"Thanks, Sis. I confer unto you the highest of praises, yo."

Thea had to hurriedly gulp down the pastry before she ended up choking on it. "You're...welcome? I take it this means your conversation went well?"

"Yep, and it's all thanks to you."

Annette gleefully plopped herself down right beside Thea. Matilda was almost too far away to see, but Annette had yet to take her eyes off of her.

"You know, Annette..."

"Yeah?"

"Once I was actually separated from my parents, too. It was only for four weeks for me, but still."

Compared to what Annette had been through, that hardly even registered. There were probably plenty of girls in Lamplight who'd gone through far more hardships than she had.

However, the lonely fear she felt back then still stung.

Just as the light from the hero who saved her lingered in her heart, so, too, did that painful emotion.

"What about it, yo?"

"...Nothing, I suppose."

Annette didn't need to hear her story. There was no reason to force her to listen.

Annette's situation and Thea's past didn't have anything to do with each other.

"I would like to hear your answer, though." Thea took Annette's hands in hers. "What is it you want to do? Do you want to save Matilda, or do you—?"

Angry shouts rose up from over by the main road.

Out of the corner of her eye, she could see emergency vehicles and police officers rushing as fast as they could.

Did something happen? What could it be, I wonder?

It wasn't anything worth panicking over.

In a city like this, monstrous crimes were a fairly regular occurrence.

"......"

Annette's eyes were as wide as saucers.

Thea immediately realized what she was so alarmed about.

"It's okay, Annette." She gently rubbed her teammate's hand. "That's not the direction of Matilda's hotel."

"........."

"There's nothing to worry about. I'm sure she's fine."

Hearing Annette's silence was enough to give Thea her answer. Annette had no desire to abandon Matilda to her fate.

Thea stroked her head. "You should just go ahead and do whatever it is you want to do."

"Sis—" For a moment, the words refused to come out. "Why are you doing all this for me, yo?"

There were plenty of answers that came to mind.

After all, Monika had asked her the same question—though, in her case, it was with a good deal more exasperation.

Was it because they were teammates? To live up to an ideal? Basic deference to societal norms?

No, it wasn't any of that. Thea couldn't explain away her actions with anything nearly so neat or tidy.

"Because when I look at you, it makes me want to have your back."

That feeling welled up from deep inside her. She couldn't have ignored it if she'd wanted to.

"Now, can you tell me what *you* want? You can be as selfish as you'd like, I promise."

Annette sucked in a big breath.

"I wanna save my mom, yo!"

Thea gave the shouted answer a big nod. "All right. I'll work something out, then."

That was a big decision Annette had just made. A choice far harsher than any fourteen-year-old should have to shoulder.

That meant the rest was up to Thea.

She was going to have to break through the nightmare that was closing in on them and save her teammate the way a hero would.

A series of shops and restaurants sat clustered around the base of a series of mega-hotels.

The ones facing the main street were welcoming and well maintained, but all it took was a single step into the side alleys before the establishments one found became decidedly seedier. One moment, you could be passing by a nightclub that catered to excited tourists, and the next, you found yourself standing in front of a sketchy "pharmacy" with your nose assailed by the smell of the countless discarded cigarettes lining the wayside.

Even in the wee hours of the night, finding a store with its lights still on was a trivial affair. There were plenty of people out and about, some of them trying to win over women in bars and others making the bets of their lives in underground casinos.

Thea felt an odd sort of empathy toward them.

She slipped out of the hotel and headed down the road alongside Monika.

That night, they had chosen to lodge at a much cheaper establishment than the first-class hotel they'd been staying at previously. Part of it was because they were trying to lay low, but the decision had come about largely on account of the sorry state of their wallets. Despite the fact that they were a pair of teenage girls slinking about in the dead of night, nobody paid them a second thought.

Monika glared at her. "Just how far do you plan on taking me?"

A mere ten minutes prior, Monika had out-and-out threatened her.

In their hotel room, she'd held Thea at gunpoint and asked her if she was going to betray Lamplight.

Thea responded by suggesting that they go somewhere else so they didn't wake Erna and Annette, and the two of them headed away from the nighttime crowd.

Eventually, they reached an abandoned alleyway.

Under the streetlight's dim glow, Thea spoke. "I want to talk this over."

The alley sat at about six and a half feet wide in the space between two buildings.

The loud echo from Thea's voice reverberated off the building walls.

"...Well, that's disappointing." Monika stretched her arms toward the sky. "But hey, I guess that's all you're good for."

"The thing is, I don't think either of us is wrong." Thea faced Monika as she made her statement. "Both of us have something we refuse to back down on, and both of us are acting in accordance with that belief. I want to save the people who need saving, even if it means bending the rules. You want to do what's right for the group, and you won't accept any exceptions to that. Don't you see? We're coming at this from different sides, but I think we can both find something to respect in the other."

"Is that all you wanted to say? 'Cause you still haven't given me much of a reason to care." Monika cracked her neck in boredom. "Out with it already. Are you going to turn Matilda in, or are you betraying the team?"

Those were the two nightmarish options Thea had available to her.

Choosing the former would mean discarding Annette's feelings, and the latter would lead to her own destruction.

There was only one way out.

"I'm choosing the third option."

"The what?"

"It's simple. I'm going to make you surrender. All I have to do is shut you up, and then we won't have to turn Matilda over, and nobody will know about our crime."

Thea gracefully made her declaration.

"Both of us are right, so there's only one way forward—we fight it out."

That was the path she'd chosen.

She was going to defeat Monika with her own two hands.

Even if Monika declined her challenge, she would just attack her anyway.

Thea had come there with the resolve to never back down.

"You get fifty out of a hundred for that answer." Monika's lips curled. Her expression was so confident she almost seemed happy. "Good stuff, Thea. This might be the first thing you've ever done that I respected."

She withdrew three rubber balls from her pocket, then held them between the fingers of her right hand as she brandished a knife with her left.

"Woulda been worth another five if you'd just attacked me by surprise. You really think you can take me head-on?" She narrowed her eyes. "Remind me, who was it who let us pass Teach's test? Who was it who took on Corpse when you were trembling too badly to move? Who was it who figured out who Matilda really was?"

"Obviously I know how strong you are. That's why I wanted to talk things out—"

"The problem with talking is you only get to do that if you're in the same league as someone. And you? You're *beneath me*."

"____"

A chill ran down Thea's spine. It was hard to believe that that intensity was coming from someone around her age.

I really didn't want to make an enemy out of you.

Monika's inscrutability didn't stop at her aloof personality and her prodigious talents.

There was also her special ability—and the fact that Thea had no idea what it was.

Every girl on Lamplight was an extreme specialist. Whether it was poisons, disguises, or stealing, each of them had a skill so honed that not even elite spies could imitate them. And Monika was no exception.

The problem was that Monika had never told them what it was.

She had gone out of her way to keep it a secret from her own teammates, and for some reason, Klaus had allowed her to do so.

That alone was proof enough of how preeminent her skills must be.

Thea smiled, then snapped her fingers. "Then, I hope you don't mind if I don't hold back."

With that, the duel between the two allies began.

Thea's first move…was to fall back a step and take shelter behind a man.

"Sorry about this, miss. Queen's orders."

"Say what?"

All of a sudden, a pair of brawny men had appeared in the back alley with them.

The two were positioned on opposite sides of Monika, trapping her in between. Earlier that afternoon, Thea had used her negotiation skills to recruit them onto her side as muscle. Most of the time, they worked as bodyguards in a gang, and they had lead pipes in their hands alongside their cruel smiles.

"You little..." Monika gave Thea a disparaging look. "Last time I checked, duels weren't supposed to involve calling in a pair of dudes to beat your opponent up for you."

"You think I'm going to pull my punches when you're so obviously out of my league?"

"You're a filthy slut."

"I'll choose to take that as a compliment."

Thea knew she was no match for Monika in a fight.

To make up for that, she was going to use every trick she had at her disposal. She tenderly caressed one of the men's backs as she whispered to them.

"Now, I have a *special* reward in mind for whoever takes her down. Ducky, I'll be your kindergarten teacher for you and tell you what a good boy you are in baby talk. Bubbles, I've got a pair of boots I wore for three days straight just waiting for me to step on you with them. And remember, boys... I'm the only one who knows your deepest, darkest desires, and I'm the only one who can make them all come true."

The men's bodies shivered like they'd been struck by lightning. They brandished their lead pipes.

"Gah! I'm surrounded by pervs!" Monika yelped.

The men ignored her and charged at her.

When a pair of men armed with lead pipes attacked them from both sides, most people would be lucky to even escape with their lives.

Aside from the shout, though, Monika was calm. She charged right back at her would-be assailants.

As she did, she hurled her rubber balls at the wall. Their black color allowed them to melt into the darkness and vanish, and the next thing Thea saw were the balls rebounding back and crashing straight into the sides of two men's heads.

Getting hit from their blind spots caught the men off guard, and Monika took full advantage of the opening that gave her.

She smashed her dagger's hilt onto the first man's jaw.

"One down."

Seeing her fight was like watching a magic trick.

True to her word, Monika's attack sent the man reeling. He collapsed onto his back, unconscious.

As he did, the other man charged at Monika from behind. However, one of her rubber balls bounced yet again and smashed him right in the face. He lost his balance, allowing Monika to dodge his attack and send him flying with a kick to the flank.

In shock, Thea watched Monika perform her superhuman feats from a safe distance.

How are the balls doing that? They're so accurate it's like they're being pulled by some force...

Annette had made those balls specially for her out of metal cores coated in rubber.

They bounced well, and the damage they could dish out made them a pretty intimidating projectile weapon. There was just one problem with them...

...Accurately hitting people with their rebounds shouldn't be possible.

If Monika was just throwing them directly at people, that would be one thing, but she wasn't. The attacks she'd launched at the men's blind spots had taken at least two bounces to get there.

Thea still didn't know what her specialty was exactly, but now she at least had a rough idea.

Monika had the ability to accurately calculate angles, trajectories, and timing as well as the aiming skills to put those calculations to use.

"But...the brainpower and fine motor control that must take!"

Her talents exceeded Thea's wildest expectations.

The man Monika kicked charged valiantly back into the fray.

"For the queen!"

"I don't want any part of this kinky shit you've got going on."

However, he froze halfway toward her like he'd hit an invisible wall.

His expression was one of complete bewilderment, and Thea didn't understand what was going on, either.

The alley was shrouded in darkness, but there were thin lines gleaming under its dim streetlight—wires. They were tangled around the man's arm. Between that and his already-ensnared right arm and left leg, he was rendered immobile.

They must have been attached to the rubber balls. As the balls bounced off the walls and ground, they had laid a net throughout the alley.

All the man could do was struggle like a butterfly caught in a spiderweb.

"And that's the second."

Monika smacked her hilt into the man's chin and downed him the same way she had the first.

It had taken her less than a minute to defeat the both of them.

"Just for the record, is that the only trick you've got up your sleeve?" Monika went around and retrieved her rubber balls off the ground. "Because if it is, this isn't gonna make for much of a fight. Come on, at least use your gun or something."

"Someone's certainly feeling high and mighty..."

Thea knew full well that she couldn't go around firing off shots while the city was crawling with soldiers. And besides, the men were far from the only trick she'd prepared.

She turned her back on her opponent and ran with all her might. She needed to lure Monika after her.

Just as Thea planned, Monika immediately gave chase. There was no way she didn't realize it was a trap, so her plan must have been to break through it head-on. Her pride refused to allow her to fall back.

In terms of athletic ability, Monika had a considerable edge.

Right when Monika was about to catch up with her, Thea slapped the back of her knife against an exposed water pipe by the side of the street. The tiny impact was enough to cause the pipe to burst, spraying a powerful jet of water directly at Monika.

"____"

She heard Monika click her tongue.

Her foe had no choice but to dodge backward to avoid the blast. "Right. You made Erna into one of your little pawns."

"'Collaborators,' please."

The pipe had already been on the verge of bursting. Erna knew about all the little seeds of misfortune lying around the city... Although in some cases, she had found out about them firsthand.

"And don't forget about Annette, too."

Thea flipped the switch she'd been keeping hidden in her pocket.

The moment she hit the button, the bricks by Monika's feet—or rather, the bombs that had been made to *look* like bricks—exploded. Tiny shards of stone shot up at her like a shotgun blast.

Monika responded by flipping her hood like a cloak, deftly parrying the small rocks.

So close. If Monika had just been a little slower, she would have taken a pretty serious blow.

No matter, though. Thea still had bucketloads of traps Erna and Annette had prepared for her.

"The truth is: This fight is three against one. Did you enjoy that taste of Annette's and Erna's powers?"

Monika wiped the dust and debris off her hood. "What a pain."

Thea didn't feel an ounce of shame about what she was doing.

After all, going around negotiating with people and getting them on her side was simply the way she did battle.

Her preparations were impeccable. She had explosives masquerading as bricks, water pipes that would rupture at the slightest impact, gas weapons hidden in metal barrels, gutters swarming with vicious rats... Thanks to the two powerful allies she'd obtained, her position in that alley was unassailable.

"Look, just surrender. I don't want to hurt you any more than I have to."

"Oh? But we were just getting to the good part." Monika's expression was utterly unflappable.

Despite the overwhelmingly unfavorable position she was in, she clearly had no intention of surrendering.

"...Honestly, I don't even know why you're the one fighting me on this," Thea murmured in dismay.

The comment wasn't part of some strategy. Those were her honest feelings.

Never once had Thea felt any passion for espionage from Monika. All she ever did was make cynical comments and belittle her teammates.

"You're always looking down on us, picking fights, throwing cruel, heartless arguments around..."

Thea glared at her.

"...Why do you even bother staying with Lamplight at all?"

"And why should I have to explain myself to someone weaker than me?"

Thea had meant what she asked, but Monika merely flicked her arm instead of answering. Something slid out of her sleeve and fell into her hand, and she hurled it with utmost efficiency.

Is she going for a ricochet attack again?

Monika had taken the two men out by bouncing rubber balls into their blind spots. Was she planning on repeating the same trick?

I've seen it too many times, though. It won't work on me anymore.

Thea braced herself and slid her hand across her remote.

"That's enough. If you keep resisting, I'll have no choice but to activate all the—"

"Too late. I can see 'em all."

Operating a hair faster than Annette's bombs could go off, Monika began taking evasive maneuvers.

It was like she could predict the future. There was no other way to put it.

Thea didn't know what was going on, but she could tell that Monika was doing something new.

She needed to get out of there now.

The moment she turned back around to flee, she spotted something unfamiliar in her peripheral vision.

Is that...a mirror?

That was exactly what it was, and it sat half embedded in the wall.

It hadn't been there a few seconds ago. That must have been what Monika just threw.

I get it. So that's how Monika figured out where all the traps—

Then her train of thought was rudely interrupted.

All of a sudden, everything went white. It was light—a powerful flash of light, reflecting off the mirror straight into her eyes.

She calculated the angle to bounce the light off the mirror!

Unable to see, she stopped in her tracks.

The next attack came at her abdomen.

"Game over. You fail on all counts." Monika, who had finally caught up to her, plunged her fist deep into Thea's solar plexus.

The remote tumbled out of Thea's hand, and her body crumpled powerlessly onto the alleyway.

She's too strong.

There were so many ways she could ricochet her attacks. So many ways she could hunt her foes down. The number of techniques at her disposal was on a whole different level.

Thea was helpless to do anything but clutch her stomach and pant as she tried to endure the pain.

"I wish you'd at least used your gun." She could hear Monika's bored voice coming from above her head. "This didn't even make for decent training."

"Training...?"

"I've been itching to get better. You know, after I lost to Corpse and all."

Thea couldn't find any words to reply.

She had been relieved that they got through the mission at all, and yet at the same time, Monika had been frustrated that it hadn't gone even better.

It's like she and I exist on different planes altogether.

She gritted her teeth.

After all the prep work she'd put in, she was still no match for Monika.

However, she couldn't afford to give up just yet.

I have to get away... I underestimated how much better she was than me, and these tricks aren't going to be enough to beat her...

Still down on her hands and knees, she readied her knife and took a swipe at Monika's legs. Monika dodged the way Thea knew she would, but at least it kept her at bay.

Thea gathered strength in her legs and rose back to her feet. She needed to put some distance between herself and Monika. Even a little would be better than nothing.

Then she felt something grab her arm as tight as a vice. She felt like she even heard her bones creak a little.

"You think you're getting away?"

Monika wasn't about to show mercy.

She yanked Thea's arm and slammed her against the wall, causing Thea to hit her head. Everything went blurry for a moment, and she collapsed back onto the ground.

Victory was hopeless. Out of all the girls in Lamplight, Monika's skills were head and shoulders above all the others'.

Grete could give her a run for her money when it came to ingenuity, but as soon as things got physical, she would fold on the spot. Similarly, Sybilla could probably take her in a fair fight, but all Monika needed to beat her was some deception.

She was a top-of-the-class all-rounder with no weaknesses.

She was the strongest girl in Lamplight, the force that allowed their band of washouts to keep striving forward.

She was their unbeatable ace in the hole.

"That's why I wanted so badly for you to appreciate me." Before Thea knew it, she was speaking aloud. "After all, I was always the one who appreciated your talents the most..."

"You're trying to appeal to my emotions now? That's just sad."

Thea's do-or-die attempt at supplication had no effect on her. What else could she do?

If she lost here, Annette's feelings would be discarded like so much garbage, and Annette's mother would die.

For Thea, though, there was no guarantee she'd even be able to get back on her feet. Turning the tables was a distant fantasy.

Monika gave her an icy look. "...You still think you can fight? I'm pretty sure we know who the winner is by now. Or what, am I going to have to actually kill you to get it through that thick skull of yours?"

The homicidal energy Monika was giving off chilled Thea to her core.

Her knees trembled, and tears nearly welled up in her eyes.

I just... I need to get away... If I can just catch her in a trap this time, I can—

As her thoughts turned, a dreary voice echoed in her mind.

"You're trying to back down? Now? ...Pathetic."

It was Corpse, snickering.

And he was right. When faced with a powerful foe, all she'd been able to do was cower in fear.

"God, you're even soft on yourself."

Later, Monika had criticized her in much the same way. Sure enough, that was the unvarnished truth. Thea's mental fortitude was abysmal.

But what choice do I have? Unlike Monika, I'm not even armed.

And her ability wasn't going to let her close the skill gap, either.

After all, locking eyes for three seconds? Did she really think her opponent was going to give her that kind of time in the middle of a fight?

"If you hone that special talent of yours, you'll be the strongest spy around."

Then it was Hearth's voice she heard in her head.

"............"

"You need to become a hero."

Thea bit down on her lip.

She could feel some sort of emotion welling up inside her.

"...You really need to work on your mental fortitude."

The final voice that echoed within her was Klaus's.

When her heart had been on the verge of breaking, he had given her a piece of advice.

"Enjoy that discord."

Now she remembered what he had told her.

"The best approach is to butt heads with your teammates directly."

"_____!"

She roused herself into action.

After summoning the strength to stand, she reached for Monika's neck with both hands.

"Are you seriously trying to *strangle* me?"

Her plan to catch Monika by surprise worked. However, Monika easily came up with a counter.

"You're not beating me in a contest of strength, I can guarantee you that." Monika snagged both of her wrists out of the air.

Now their arms were linked, leaving them jostling for position with brute force alone.

Thea lacked the power to compete with Monika's core strength, and her arms stopped short before getting to Monika's neck. She pushed as hard as she could, but she couldn't even get close.

"C'mon, slut. Just give up while you're behind."

"A hero *never* gives up."

As Thea's arms began to tremble, a small smile flitted across her face. She knew exactly how she could win.

She needed to do something Monika would never expect, and she needed to butt heads with her directly.

Fortunately, she had a weapon on hand capable of doing both at once. Hearth had told her to hone it, and hone it she had.

"You're going to regret the day you ever crossed a slut."

It was time to butt heads. Directly.

The moment Thea's arms were about to give out, she dropped the hammer.

"I'm code name Dreamspeaker—and it's time to lure them to their ruin."

She released all the force she'd been pushing into her arms.

Then she spread them out wide and thrust her head straight at Monika's face.

But not for a headbutt.

Their noses smashed into each other, and right as they did, Thea planted her lips firmly on Monika's.

"_____!"

Monika's eyes went wide.

Lovers sometimes closed their eyes when they shared a romantic kiss, but this kiss was anything but. This hijacking of her lips would make anyone's eyes go wide, especially if the kiss came paired with the pain from a headbutt.

And when that happened, *it would invariably provide an opening to meet their gaze*!

Even Monika couldn't help but get thrown for a loop. Her body went stiff.

A few moments later, she started to thrash about, but Thea used every drop of strength in her body to hold her teammate's head still.

Eventually, Monika summoned up enough power to forcefully shove Thea off her. Thea slammed into the wall.

"I'll kill you I'll kill you I'll kill you I'll kill you I'll kill you I'll kill you I'll kill you I'll kill you I'll kill you I'll kill you I'll kill you I'll kill you I'll kill you I'll kill you!" Monika shouted at a mile a minute as she wiped her lips clean. "I'll kill you, dammit!"

She hadn't used her gun throughout their entire duel, but she drew it now and shoved it in Thea's face.

With her back against the wall, Thea slid to a seat on the ground.

She couldn't move. She'd used up everything she had, and if Monika wanted to shoot her, she didn't have the strength to stop her anymore. She would simply die and be branded a filthy traitor.

However, she wasn't afraid. The fight was already decided.

"Goodness, are you really…"

Her voice rang loud and clear.

"…in love?"

Monika froze.

Her body was so stiff it was like time itself had stopped.

"………You…" Words dribbled from her mouth. She was barely coherent. "Did you—?"

Seeing her agitation was so funny that Thea let out a chuckle.

At long last, she had finally touched Monika's heart.

Now she knew the secret that Monika had kept concealed behind so many walls. She knew what made her tick.

"Were there hints I overlooked, I wonder? The romance novels, maybe? No, I suppose not." Thea shook her head as she thought back on Monika's actions. "You went out of your way to hide it so completely that no one would ever notice your precious love. And why? Well, that's simple. It was because the other person was someone close by."

She had successfully met Monika's eyes for three seconds, and doing so had revealed an emotion she never would have expected from her.

All that time, Monika had been hiding desire deep within her heart.

Monika's face flushed in despair.

"Wow, you actually look like a human being for once. I think it's a lovely look on you."

Then Thea pounded the final nail in her coffin.

"The person you love is *someone in Lamplight*, isn't it?"

Monika let out a quiet murmur. "I'll kill you…" The words spilled feebly from her mouth.

But Thea was past being afraid of her threats.

"No, you won't. After all, think of how sad that would make them."

Monika's words were nothing more than a negotiation tactic.

She had no intention whatsoever of killing Thea. There was no point in taking her threats seriously.

"That's why you wanted to get rid of Matilda. It was so you could protect Lamplight, the place your crush called home. If we helped her out, Lamplight could come under fire for aiding an Imperial spy."

The reason Monika had been so insistent that they turn Matilda in was simple.

Thea had assumed that her decision had simply been cold and calculated, but that wasn't it at all. All that time, Monika's sole priority had been one single member of their team.

That was what drove her to act as rationally as she could to ensure Lamplight's survival.

Thea nodded. "You're really single-minded in your love, aren't you?"

The moment the words left her mouth, Monika leaped at her and grabbed Thea's throat to forcibly shut her up.

Then she squeezed down with a rage far beyond anything she'd shown earlier.

"Stop that!" she barked threateningly. "Stop doing whatever you want with my heart!"

Her voice was halfway between a bellow and shriek.

When Monika loosened her grip on Thea's throat, Thea readily agreed.

"Of course. You won't hear another word out of me." Monika had gone to great lengths to hide her love; Thea wanted to honor that decision. "But I need your help."

"........."

"I have nothing but respect for your feelings. Now, I'm asking you to consider mine." She went on. "What would the person you care about want? Do you think they would really approve of leaving Matilda to die?"

"........................."

Monika went silent. After letting go of Thea's neck, she simply stood there, stock-still.

If Monika refused to play along, Thea would have no choice but to use her love against her and blackmail her with it. Doing that ran the risk of sending Monika into such a rage that she would kill Thea, but if she did that, then having committed fratricide would prevent her love from ever bearing fruit.

The two of them were on equal footing. They had fought, they had butted heads directly, and at long last, they had finally reached even ground.

" ....Shit."

At the end of the protracted silence, a frustrated murmur reached Thea's ears.

It was so faint that if she hadn't been listening closely, she might not have caught it at all.

"I have conditions." Monika let out a long exhale and raised a single finger. "One, you don't tell anyone else about my secret."

"Of course. I won't bring it up again, and I won't try to figure out who it is."

Thea was curious, of course, but she was just going to have to live with that.

Monika raised a second finger. "Two, if it looks like the army is going to catch on to what you're doing, I'm turning Matilda over on the spot. This one is nonnegotiable. I have to protect Lamplight."

"Please, be my guest." If anything, Thea would *rather* that Monika kept an eye on them.

Monika raised a third finger. "Three."

"That seems like a lot of conditions."

"...About *that*."

"Hmm?"

At that point, Monika started to get evasive. "I mean, it's kinda... Well, you get it."

"I'm afraid I really don't. What is it? You're going to have to make yourself clearer."

Monika's cheeks went ever so slightly flush.

Eventually, she awkwardly got the words out.

" ....Look, just don't tell anyone you kissed me, all right?"

It took everything Thea had not to burst into laughter.

Getting to hear Monika talk in that kind of tone wasn't something that happened every day.

"I'll take it into consideration."

"You want to get back to that fight, then?"

"I'm kidding, I'm kidding. If I had to fight you again, I'm sure I would end up in the ground."

"If you can agree to those three conditions..." Monika took a breath. "...then fine, I'll surrender."

She raised her hands in the air.

"Magnificent."

For some reason, she chose to mimic Klaus.

Thea let out a long breath and looked up at the night sky. All the exhaustion was hitting her at once.

She didn't feel like she'd surpassed Monika. Not one bit.

It had taken painstaking preparation, a specific time and place, and a favorable set of circumstances, and even then, all Thea had been able to do was bring Monika to the negotiation table. Even during the height of their battle, Monika clearly hadn't been giving it her all.

However, Thea's heart was full to bursting with all sorts of emotions.

She had finally taken a win off of Monika, and for now, that would have to do.

Thea and Monika headed back to their hotel walking side by side.

As they did, Monika muttered a brief comment. "Honestly, I wasn't even the right person for the job." Thea didn't understand what she meant. She looked over at Monika, and Monika elaborated a little. "Klaus already said it, but differences between allies really are the key to a good team. I know that as well as anyone. The problem is, none of us in Lamplight have a ruthless bone in our bodies."

"You might be right about that."

"We're too soft. The fact of the matter is: I should be the one putting a stop to all this—personal feelings be damned."

"........."

"Even if it meant I had to break your legs."

"Couldn't you come up with a nicer way to stop me?"

"This is going to bite us in the ass someday," Monika muttered. "Eventually, we'll run into an opponent who takes advantage of how soft we are."

Her fears were legitimate. Now that they'd gotten this far, Thea could calmly take her analysis for what it was worth. This wasn't Monika being rude, it was her genuinely pointing out a shortcoming they had as a team.

Thea was well aware of how far off she was from the model of a "standard" spy.

Furthermore, she had a hard time imagining any of her teammates being able to kill someone without hesitation, either. As far as weaknesses went, that was a pretty serious one.

When Klaus wasn't there, someone needed to be able to step up and harden their heart where the others couldn't.

For now, though, there was only one thing Thea had to say.

"The thing is, Monika, I don't think the role of bad guy suits you all that well."

"Ex*cuse* me?" Monika snapped in irritation. "And why's that?"

"Because I've seen what's in your heart. You're no good at squashing your emotions."

There was no way Monika could ever truly become cruel. Try as she might, her true emotions would always end up leaking back through.

She had tried so, so hard to conceal her single-minded love.

Anyone who held an emotion that strong wouldn't be able to help themselves from empathizing with people.

"Back at the restaurant, you went out of your way to help Annette get dressed up nicely. Say what you like, you'll never be able to get rid of that compassion."

Monika sped up her pace in embarrassment.

"...Yeah, and that's why we have such a problem," Thea heard her mutter gloomily.

By the sound of it, keeping her emotions fully in check was a task beyond even her.

When the two of them got back to their hotel room, they found their previously sleeping teammates, Annette and Erna, wide awake.

Hearing them leave the room earlier had woken them up. They must have been pretty worried, as for once, they were sitting peacefully on the bed without so much as quarreling.

"Big Sis Thea, Big Sis Monika!" Erna said the moment she spotted them. "Are you okay?"

Beside her, Annette just stared at them in nervous silence.

Thea gave them the gentlest smile she could muster.

"Everything's fine. Monika agreed to help us save Matilda."

Annette cheered and leaped at Monika. "Yay! Sis!"

Monika nimbly evaded her assault. "Quit trying to jump on me; I'm in a bad mood."

"Come on, don't be shy! I wanna give you a kiss, yo!"

"I've gone through enough trauma for one evening already, thanks."

When Annette started making a kissy face, Monika redoubled her efforts to get away from her. The two of them went on a wild rampage around the room, but something told Thea that the two of them were more compatible than they let on.

Soon they would embark on an operation to save Matilda.

However, there was one thing Thea need to check first. As things stood, Erna was under no obligation to take part in the steps to come.

When she conveyed that thought aloud—

"I have a condition, too."

—Erna gave her reply.

"Is giving conditions some sort of fad these days?"

Thea had just finished doing the same thing to Monika.

Erna briskly thrusted her index finger forward. "Annette, you have to stop bullying me."

She pointed at Annette, who was still trying to plant her lips on Monika.

"If you can do that...and if you start being my f-f-friend, then I'll help, too."

By the end, Erna was talking a mile a minute.

"..............."

After zoning out in confusion for a bit, Annette cocked her head to the side. "I thought we were friends this whole time, though."

"..........!"

Erna's face reddened.

It looked like she would be joining the operation as well.

At five o'clock the next morning, the four girls headed to Matilda's hotel.

Fortunately, she hadn't been caught yet.

However, a dirt-cheap hotel room was no place to hold a clandestine discussion. They took Matilda back to a secluded spot on the coastline.

Thea and the others were supposed to have gone home already, and Matilda blinked at them in surprise upon discovering that they were still in town.

Annette was the one who broke the ice.

"Mom, you have to retire as a spy."

Naturally, Matilda froze in shock. "What...?"

"Annette is right. We need you to promise you'll quit." Thea was done second-guessing herself. "As you might have surmised, the four of us are spies working for the Republic."

"So wait, we're...competitors?"

"Exactly. We can't lend a hand to an enemy spy, even if they're the mother of a friend. You need to retire, effective immediately. If you can promise us that, we'll help you get over the border."

Matilda's mouth hung slightly agape as she let out a delighted sigh. That must have come as a great relief to her. When she noticed how harsh Thea's gaze was, though, she quickly cast her eyes downward.

"But...how? Do you have secret connections, or—?"

"Nope. We're going to be doing it the hard way."

Their lives would have been so much easier if they had someone on the inside like that.

Here, the only people they had to rely on were each other. They couldn't even get Klaus or their other teammates involved.

"The plan is simple: The five of us are going to break through the army's siege."

As Matilda stared at her dumbfoundingly, Thea told her when and where she needed to be for the plan to start, then left.

After they walked a short way, Monika shot her a question to double-check something. "So you didn't end up telling Klaus about the situation?"

"Of course not." Thea laughed. "He would never go along with something like this."

Monika shrugged. "He's probably pretty worried about us, then. It's morning, and we still aren't back."

Thea nodded.

She'd considered calling Klaus and making up some excuse for their tardiness, but she'd ultimately decided against it. With his intuition, he'd be able to see through any lie she told him. The only way to keep Matilda safe was to not call him at all.

"Then he'll just have to be worried," Thea replied. "It's time for us to disappear."

Monika nodded. "That's harsh. But you know what? I can get behind it."

Erna smiled. "The four of us will go missing."

Annette hummed a little tune. "We're like lost children, yo."

And with that, the girls disappeared so they could go on their secret mission—the mission that not even their teacher could know about.

It was early in the morning, and the sun was just starting to crest the horizon.

A long, long day was about to start in the entertainment district.

It was five AM when the girls decided to help Matilda escape.

They had no way of knowing it, but Klaus and Lily would reach the station at noon.

And there was something else they had no way of knowing as well.

At three PM, Klaus's warning to Welter was going to come true—a villain would arrive at the city's port.

Interlude

Missing ④

When three PM rolled around, and the sun began its descent downward, Klaus found a lead on the missing girls.

The city was home to a multi-tenant building, which was three stories tall and had a single semibasement. The first floor was a bookie's office where you could bet on horse races by proxy, the second floor had a moneylender, and the top floor had a sign for the sketchiest print shop imaginable. Nothing about the building was especially wholesome. Klaus didn't see a sign posted for the semibasement, so he surmised that whoever worked out of it probably wanted to avoid attention.

At present, the building was sealed off and surrounded by soldiers. He could see Welter standing inside with a puzzled expression.

Klaus pushed his way through the police tape and joined him. "Looks like there was a murder here."

Welter looked up, then scowled. "*You.* Didn't you say you were leaving?"

"You seriously believed a lie that obvious?"

Klaus glanced around at the bloodstains. A lot of blood had been shed in that room.

"There were five people dead," Welter said. "The police report said it was probably a fight between two gangs, but if you took the time to come here yourself, then I take it there's an intelligence angle?"

"Dammit, I told the police to hush the whole incident up."

"Quit trying to get rid of me." Welter clicked his tongue. "The killer set a booby trap with piano wire. It was a nasty piece of work—one that required a lot of skill to set up. All five of the victims got sliced to ribbons, and the corpses were pretty ugly. From what I hear, they had trouble even telling which pieces went with which bodies."

"That much is clear from the crime scene. Our culprit did a pretty brutal job here."

The room was practically drenched in blood. The bodies had already been cleared away, but the fact that there were bloodstains reaching all the way up to the ceiling told a clear enough story of how gory it had been.

"It's the same MO as the spy we're hunting," Welter noted.

The spy in question was the one who'd killed a Lylat Kingdom agent and was currently on the run.

As Klaus turned his thoughts to the woman's true identity, a sharp aroma hit his nose.

"That's odd," he murmured. "There's a lingering scent of tear gas in the air, but it wasn't sprayed on the day of the crime."

"Hmm? What do you mean?"

"The day before the murders, someone filled the room with tear gas."

That would mean that office had been attacked not once, but twice. Three days ago, it had been full of tear gas, and it wasn't until late the night after that the enemy spy went on her piano wire rampage.

Welter furrowed his brow in confusion. "The police say that the five dead people were a group of criminals. They started with petty theft, then branched out to every crime under the sun. People like them tend to make a lot of enemies."

"..............Ah, so that's what happened."

Klaus nodded.

He headed for the exit. He'd learned everything he was going to learn there.

"Hold on, Bonfire." However, Welter stopped him in his tracks. "What is it you just figured out?"

"That I'm no use here. This case is beyond me."

"That's another lie, isn't it?"

Welter leveled a fierce glare at him. Then he told his men to clear the room. The soldiers weren't about to disobey an order from their captain, so they did as they were told and exited the semibasement.

Welter and Klaus were the only ones left in the office.

"I haven't seen Torchlight around lately," Welter remarked. "How's he doing?"

That code name belonged to Klaus's mentor—Guido.

"Oh, he's fine. Too fine, if anything."

"His close combat skills are alive and well, then. I got him to agree to spar with me once, you know. He destroyed me, of course, but he said I had good fundamentals. That's something I'll always be proud of."

"What are you trying to say?"

"That I'm not some rookie. I pick up on things, too." Welter's voice grew sterner. "I can feel a great evil in the air."

"A what?"

"The truly evil masquerade as saints. They wear righteous smiles, manipulating those ignorant to their nature while they destroy anyone their hearts tell them to. There's a great evil at work here, Bonfire— someone so wicked their soul is twisted to its core."

"........."

"It's the military's job to put people like that down. Now, tell me everything you know."

A sense of justice as firm as steel burned in his eyes as he looked straight at Klaus. It was that firm will—that pride he took in crushing evil wherever it stood—that had allowed someone as young as him to rise to the rank of captain.

It was that evil he'd sensed that had driven him to gather as many troops as he had.

Klaus shook his head. "You don't see it, do you?"

"Wh—?"

"Your sense of duty is admirable; I'll give you that. But understand that I have my position to consider as well. Make sure you stay out of my way."

Welter's face went bright red. His fists trembled. "You damn spies think you're all that... The army's just one big joke to you people, isn't it?"

"Oh, and one more piece of advice," Klaus said dispassionately. "Don't chase the spy into the sea. Wouldn't want them to slip away, you know?"

That was the most important piece of counsel Klaus had given him yet.

Welter, however, took it as an insult. If looks could kill, Klaus would have died on the spot.

"There you go picking fights again…"

When Klaus left the semibasement, Lily greeted him with a look of utter exasperation. She'd been stealthily watching the whole exchange.

"Give me some credit," Klaus replied. "When I pick a fight, it's always for a reason."

"It is? What did you do it for, then?"

"To piss him off."

"That makes it worse!"

"As things stand, they're in a pretty unfavorable position. I needed to throw the CO off his game a bit."

Even so, they were in for a rough battle. However, Klaus was just going to have to believe in them.

Lily tilted her head to the side. She clearly didn't understand what he meant.

Klaus decided to put off explaining himself. There was something more important he needed to tell her.

"We're putting our search for the missing four on hold for a bit."

"What?"

It sounded like they were still alive. Klaus wanted to go help them out, but there was something else that needed doing.

"Our job now is to go deal with the eventuality that our missing comrades overlooked."

Lily stared at him blankly. "You mean you've figured out what's going on?"

"Somehow or other, yes."

Klaus had some choice words to say about the outrageous decisions the girls were making. Why did his subordinates all have to be such handfuls?

He had figured out about 80 percent of the situation, and with a little more intel, he'd be able to put together the full picture.

Still, he already knew why the girls had chosen to go missing.

And he knew what the great evil Welter had referenced was, too.

Interlude

Villain

Passenger ships arrived at the city's port four times a day.

Of those, the ship that docked at three PM was a bona fide luxury liner. The massive ship was over three hundred feet long, and at full capacity, it could hold five hundred aboard. The majority of those who rode it were tourists from overseas, although their primary demographic was rich people from continents that had escaped the Great War's ravages. The fact that the war had been over for a decade meant that some of the ship's passengers were wealthy Din industrialists who had brought their businesses back to prosperity as the country rebuilt itself.

Among the bustling crowd of people waiting impatiently to disembark, one of them in particular was a good deal odder than the rest.

He was a mushroom.

The moment anyone so much as glanced at him, they would find themselves bewildered at how completely his hair made his head look like a mushroom. *God bless your poor barber,* passersby would think as they stared at him slack-jawed. The other passengers had taken to calling him Mushroom Man, and children would laugh at him when he walked by.

His hairstyle was so comical there wasn't a single person on the ship who didn't have it etched into their memory.

It was so memorable, in fact, that none of them would be able to remember a single *other* thing about his appearance.

And that was just how the Galgad spy White Spider liked it.

When White Spider stepped down onto the port, he was struck by disappointment at the city.

The area was definitely flourishing, but none of it managed to actually surpass his expectations.

He had heard it was the foremost entertainment district in all of Din, but it was certainly nothing to write home about. There were a couple mega-hotels whose designs they'd cribbed off the Empire's, nothing more. Losing the war had sent the Empire into the verge of decline, but even they had a fair handful of entertainment districts bigger and better than this. That was about all you could expect from a backwater county like Din, White Spider supposed.

Sure enough, this whole country is basically a hole in the ground.

He scratched the back of his head.

What a hassle. If only we could just ignore this dump.

At the end of the day, this kind of stuff was all that Din was capable of. Their economy was tiny, and their impact on international politics was minuscule. It would have taken a nation ten times their strength to even give the Empire pause. It hardly seemed worth it sending spies into their borders at all. During the last war, Galgad had steamrolled them like the tiny insect they were.

The problem is the crazy amount of resources they keep pumping into training spies.

The Din Republic was supposed to be a small fish in a big pond, and yet somehow, their intelligence agency—the Foreign Intelligence Office—and its spies had dealt the Empire one humiliating defeat after another.

The Empire and the Republic shared similar languages and culture, ethnicities, and even a border. If you wanted to send spies into the Empire, those were just about the best conditions you could ask for.

Time and time again, the Din Republic had stolen confidential documents from the Empire and sold them to larger nations to prop up their national budget. They acted as a sort of lookout for the Allies, and that made them a thorn in the Empire's side.

They were a backwater with a big secret—the fact that they were an espionage powerhouse.

We ripped their spy network to shreds once already, but they recovered faster than we could have imagined. They're like an infestation that just keeps coming back.

As White Spider continued musing on the relationship between the Empire and the Republic, he reached the hotel he was looking for.

There were no guards in sight. The person he was after must have successfully stayed low.

He headed for the counter, told them he wanted a room, and went upstairs. He pretended to go into the room he'd just been given, then sneaked into the room next door to it.

Inside, he found a woman lying on the bed. She looked dead tired, and she was as pale as a sheet.

She was the person White Spider was looking for. In the Empire, she went by the name Matilda.

When she noticed she had a visitor, her eyes went wide.

"A mushroom…"

"*That's* your first reaction?"

It didn't exactly inspire confidence, but at least she hadn't out-and-out screamed. In terms of skill, the Empire's spies were a mixed bag.

"So backup actually came." Matilda sighed. "They didn't abandon me after all!"

"Maybe, maybe not." White Spider shrugged. "I could just be here to kill you."

"What…?"

"You were an afterthought. The only reason I'm in this country at all is because our man Deepwater went dark. You're just a stop on my way back, and I have full authorization to kill you or help you escape as I see fit."

He pointed his gun straight at Matilda's forehead.

"What's it going to be? Can you think of any reason I should let you live?"

"……………"

"I smell blood." The stench of death was all over her. "You killed someone, right? Why? What kind of idiot goes and makes a scene like that when they're supposed to be in hiding?"

She was of no use to him.

He started to squeeze the trigger—

"Hee-hee-hee."

—and Matilda let out a peculiar laugh.

"Huh?" A wave of discomfort washed over him.

However, Matilda couldn't seem to hold in her creepy laughter.

"Hee-hee-hee. Hee-hee-hee. Heeeee-hee-hee-hee. HEEEE-HEE-HEE-HEE-HEE-HEE-HEE-HEE-HEE-HEE!"

She clamped her hands over her mouth, but her voice spilled out between her fingers.

What's wrong with this lady?

White Spider frowned, and all of a sudden, Matilda stopped laughing.

"The situation's chaaanged."

"What?"

"I can get out juuust fine, even without your help. And the killings were for revenge, but really, I just kinda waaanted to."

White Spider blinked, surprised by her voice's abrupt shift into a lazy drawl.

Matilda continued explaining. "You know, I was in reeeal trouble. I was surrounded by army scum, my tools were all stolen, and I didn't know what to do. I knew it would be dangerous, but I was thinking about trying to butcher my way through their whole army, and I was *this* close to actually going for it, too."

A disquieting smile spread readily across her face.

"But then a miracle happened. I ran into my long-lost daughter."

"Huh. Must've been a touching reunion. Good for you."

White Spider had no interest in the subject, so his responses were perfunctory at best, but Matilda went on with obvious delight. She pointed at the cobalt-blue toolbox sitting in the corner of the room.

"I used that to hit her."

"Huh?"

It was made of iron, and it looked pretty heavy.

"I hit my daughter with it again and again and again and again. I beat all the memories out of her and left her black-and-blue, and now she idolizes me and is trying to saaave me. She doesn't remember I beat her, and she even calls me Mom! She has nooooo idea that I'm just using her!"

Her smile radiated ecstasy.

"What a stupid, stuuupid girl!"

Seeing the madness in her face left White Spider speechless.
She was a monster.
He didn't know what exactly had happened, but it sounded like she'd found a way to escape that involved taking advantage of her unwitting daughter. If so, that was fine. If nothing else, it meant that there was no need for White Spider to lend her a hand.
That made his decision simple—getting involved would be a waste of time.
He lowered his gun.
"I always knew you were nasty, but I guess this time around it gets you passing marks. Just make sure you get rid of that blood stink. You reek bad enough that anyone who knows what's up could take you in an instant."
"Thanks for the heads-uuup."
"After that, do what you will. I'll be doing the same, and I'll head home when I'm good and ready."
At the end of the day, saving colleagues who were stranded alone wasn't his department. Matilda's job was important, but it wasn't like any of the information she had was particularly valuable. White Spider had meant it when he said he had stopped by as an afterthought.
On his way out, though, he realized he had a question he wanted answered.
"Don't you have *any* maternal love for the girl?"
"Not a siiingle bit." Matilda responded in the same drawl as earlier. "I mean, the kid's a creepy little brat."
No hesitation, no remorse.

The stage was set.
The four "chosen" members of Lamplight: Monika, Thea, Erna, and Annette.
The Military Intelligence Department led by Welter Barth.

Matilda, the Imperial spy plotting to make her escape by taking advantage of her daughter.

Lamplight's boss Klaus, who'd rushed over alongside Lily.

White Spider, the Imperial spy who'd intruded on the scene at the last minute.

All their conflicting plans and expectations were about to come to a head, and the banquet of espionage was about to begin.

Chapter 5

A Battle Against Great Evil

According to the weather forecast, it was supposed to rain from the middle of the night to early in the morning.

Sure enough, thick clouds began blanketing the sky over the city at around ten PM. The humidity rose, too, enough so that even just breathing was enough to make one's throat feel damp. Rain was about to start pouring at any moment.

Three battles began during that moonless night.

In two of them, shots were fired immediately.

The port's outskirts were lined with warehouses.

There were warehouses for holding imported goods next to the cargo ship docking area, and slightly farther away, there were warehouses for holding old, worn-out ships. The latter was rarely used. It was like a watercraft morgue stuffed full of broken fishing boats.

Under normal circumstances, the area would have been completely empty at ten at night.

However, things were pretty far from normal, and a group of soldiers had been stationed there to guard the area.

Captain Barth had predicted that the enemy spy was at the end of their rope and would try to force their way through, so he'd given the order for each platoon to increase their nighttime patrols. The soldiers strode around with tense faces and their rifles at the ready. However, the girls had investigated all that ahead of time.

They lurked in a boat warehouse with bated breath.

"Let's go over the plan one last time." Thea turned to the others. "The only way for us to get Matilda out is through this port. There are ways we could get her through the station or onto the highway, but as long as she's in the country, they'll keep hunting her down."

The longer it took for Matilda to make it over the border, the worse her situation would get.

She needed to get out, and she needed to get out tonight.

"There's a freighter leaving the port at eleven PM. It's already mostly loaded, but there's some final cargo that they aren't loading until later tonight. We're going to slip Matilda in among it. To do that, we're going to cause a commotion to force the dockworkers to evacuate the port and to lure the soldiers away."

Annette and Erna nodded.

Monika, who had punched a small hole in the warehouse wall and was looking through it to keep watch, spoke up.

"It's here. It's a blue iron container, and I have visual confirmation on the 3-896 on the side."

The cargo they were waiting for had arrived right on schedule.

After Thea finished reminding the group of the plan, she headed over to Matilda, who was waiting separately from the others.

"Um…" Matilda's voice rang with worry. "Is this really going to work? I mean, all this business about hiding among the cargo…"

"It wouldn't have, not historically. We used to use casks and wooden barrels, and those are too small for a person to fit into."

"That's what I was thinking…"

"Nowadays, though, even Din's starting to adopt shipping containers. The port uses them for over half its goods, and they're easily big enough to hold a person. That opens up new options for spies."

Standardization of freight had done wonders for increasing the efficiency of shipping goods, and as technology advanced, the nations of the world were becoming more connected at a blistering clip. Those connections were a breeding ground for new covert techniques.

"But…won't the soldiers be on the lookout for that kind of thing?"

"There are four different cargo ships that all depart in the same time slot. That's too many for them to check."

The other three ships weren't done being loaded, either, so the departure area was filled to bursting with containers. There was no way someone could be found after sneaking into one of them.

"And on top of that, we aren't putting you on the boat to Galgad. Your destination is going to be the Lylat Kingdom."

It stood to reason that the army would keep an extra-watchful eye on the Galgad-bound ship, but as long as Matilda broke through their net at all, she could just as easily take another route back to the Empire from there. She could handle herself once she got to Lylat.

The iron shipping container was designed not to open from the inside, so Thea handed Matilda the tool she would need to use to escape once she was in. It was a rod-shaped blowtorch about twenty inches long.

"Annette made this specially for you. It should be able to burn through an iron latch, no problem."

Annette had put it together in just a few short hours. "I made it myself, so it'll never let you down, yo!" she'd said as she gave it her stamp of approval.

Matilda clutched it like it was the most precious thing in the world. She stopped trembling.

With that, everything was in place to put the plan into action.

Thea headed back over to Monika, whose eyes had gone oddly wide. Monika sat frozen in silent contemplation. "………"

Thea wasn't quite sure what to make of her expression. "Is something the matter?" she asked.

"Nah, not really." Monika shrugged. "I was just thinking how much more you look the part than Klaus does. How's it feel, being in the commander's seat for once?"

"Like you're not going to get a rise out of me for that comment."

"I'm just saying, being CO is a big responsibility. You screwing up could mean we all get executed."

"I don't even want to think about that... But it's okay. I've made up my mind."

On hearing that, Monika waved her hand flippantly as she started walking away. "Well, that's boring."

At the moment, not even Monika's cynicism would be enough to get Thea down. "But honestly, I'm not worried."

"Oh yeah? And why's that?"

"I keep telling you, remember? With the two of us together, we're unbeatable."

Monika gave her an exasperated wave. "Thanks for the vote of confidence."

It was time.

"It's up and running, yo," Annette said.

Thea and the others headed over to the warehouse door just in time to see the white fumes rising up from the docking area. The device they'd planted that afternoon had gone off.

Thea observed the scene through her binoculars.

A group of soldiers had gathered at the docking area and was starting to evacuate the dockworkers. Powerful spotlights swept back and forth across the harbor like arms of a colossus.

Before long, all the civilians were gone. Now all they had to do was clear the soldiers out of the docking area as well.

"Well, that's not good," Monika said as she looked through her telescope.

"Yeah, I wasn't expecting so many soldiers," Thea replied.

"That's not it. You see the mirror by dock three?"

When they went there earlier, Monika had set up mirrors around the dock. They were disguised as trash, so nobody had given them a second look, and Monika was now using them to survey the entire port at once.

"No, my binoculars aren't strong enough," Thea replied. "What is it?"

"Captain Welter Barth, that's what. He's here. Apparently, he's supposed to be some sort of genius."

"Oh really? I've heard rumors that he's quite a catch, but I never knew how much of it was true."

"I don't care about his looks, but his skills are the real deal. Those soldiers are going to be well led."

If the man had earned Monika's respect, then he was surely a force to be reckoned with.

However, it didn't matter who their opponent was. They couldn't afford to back down.

Thea extended her leg to take the first step out of the warehouse—

"No, wait!"

—but Erna threw herself at her before she could, knocking Thea over onto her side.

The ground by Thea's feet burst.

Was that sniper fire?

If Erna hadn't stopped Thea the moment she sensed danger, that bullet would have hit her dead-on. Goose bumps ran across Thea's skin.

What's going on? How did they find us already, and where's the sniper shooting from?

She took cover inside the warehouse.

The bullet was buried deep in the ground. It must have been shot from a considerable distance away.

Thea went pale as confusion stirred up inside her. Was this Captain Barth's doing? No, that wasn't it. This was something else, something they hadn't foreseen.

Beside her, Erna's face was just as white as hers. It was the most scared Thea had ever seen her.

"I don't think we should go out right now," Erna said hoarsely. "I have a really, really bad feeling about it."

"Thank you, Erna." Thea patted her head. "Still, this is a bad position to be in."

They had made too much noise, and the soldiers patrolling near the ship warehouses were reacting to it. She could hear their chatter and footsteps drawing nearer.

"When it rains, it pours, huh?" Monika started reaching for the gun in her breast pocket. "What's the plan? At this rate, the soldiers are gonna box us in."

She was right. If they stayed in one place, they might not be able to get out later.

However, ignoring Erna's warning and revealing themselves to the mysterious sniper was too dangerous to be a real option.

It makes me want to say "how unlucky"...

Thea bit her lip. They were in serious trouble.

The first battle—the chosen members of Lamplight versus Welter Barth's Military Intelligence Department—had begun.

White Spider lifted his head from his scope and cocked it to the side.

"Huh? She dodged it? But how?"

His distinctive mushroom hair was hidden beneath a beanie, and his face was concealed behind a large mask. He looked suspicious as all hell, but there was nobody around to accost him.

At the moment, he was inside an unfinished hotel construction site directly beside the port. He lay prone as he aimed his gun.

Although the hotel was still under construction, he was up on what would eventually become its seventh floor. There were no walls yet, just flooring and support pillars.

The maximum range that the Empire's top-of-the-line rifles could accurately hit targets at was about a thousand feet away. However, White Spider's hotel vantage point was over triple that far from the port. Shooting from that range wouldn't normally have been possible, but White Spider had made custom modifications to his gun that allowed him to easily disassemble it for transport as well as use it as a bona fide sniper rifle.

As he held his modified long-range rifle, his thoughts turned.

When he heard Matilda's story, he made the call to forego killing her in favor of letting her go to see what she did. Something about her daughter and her daughter's friends had struck him as extremely off.

After all, spies helping a known enemy spy?

That was concerning. No decent spy would ever be that soft. What was going through their heads?

Were they inexperienced, maybe?

Now, that was a thought.

The first thing White Spider envisioned was the Republic's newly formed spy team—the one comprised of a single man and seven female academy washouts.

This was something he needed to look into.

"First things first, let's kill one of 'em and see what happens from there."

His plan had been to shoot one of them dead the moment they started carrying out their plan with Matilda.

That was why he went for the shot on the girl he'd caught a glimpse of a moment ago, but somehow, she managed to dodge it. Maybe she had sensed the danger she was in, or maybe it was something else. Either way, though, she would have to show herself again before long.

"Looks like the army's onto them, too, so they'll have to come out soon." White Spider peered through his scope. "Now, are you going to let the army surround you, or are you going to let me shoot you? Pick your poison."

White Spider's position of absolute superiority was going to allow him to reliably take down his target.

That was the way he liked to do things. He made sure to never take on risks he didn't have to.

The thing was, he was in the Din Republic, and he was staring down a group of suspicious-looking girls.

Unlikely as it was, there was one man whose path he *absolutely needed to avoid crossing*.

"Ah!"

Suddenly, he felt a wave of hostility and quickly rolled onto his back. That was close—he almost hadn't sensed it at all.

There was a tall man behind him.

"You noticed me. That means you know what you're doing."

The man stood proud and imposing.

His confidence was terrifying, as if he didn't care if White Spider turned and shot him.

"The *hell*?" White Spider screamed from the bottom of his heart. He scrambled to his feet, but his knees were still shaking.

The man gave White Spider a cold look.

"And the only people who'd react like that to seeing my face are Imperial spies."

"This is bullshit."

White Spider had etched that face into his brain.

It belonged to the most dangerous man in the whole Republic—the one enemy he absolutely couldn't afford to run into.

It belonged to the monster that they had sent operative after operative to assassinate—and who had turned the tables on all of them.

It belonged to the spy who had walked into a laboratory filled to the brim with traps and had walked right out with the bioweapon they'd stolen.

It belonged to code name Bonfire.

"No, no, this is some RAGING HORSESHIT! What the hell are *you* doing here?!"

White Spider ran. He made sure to grab his signature rifle, but he left all his other tools behind.

The encounter didn't *completely* catch him by surprise. Unlikely as it was, he'd known it was a possibility.

However, no amount of anticipation could have prepared him for how terrifying the man would be in the flesh.

White Spider barreled for the stairs as fast as his legs would carry him—

"I sealed off the stairs."

—but then he stopped in his tracks.

There was noxious, colored foam barring the sole exit.

What's with the bubbles?

They were piled up in a heap, walling off the stairs like a barricade. Someone other than Bonfire must have silently set them off.

When White Spider poked the foam, it sent a burning sensation through his skin. The foam was poisonous.

He paused. He certainly wasn't foolish enough to dive into that pool of deadly froth.

Whoever made these has gotta be one hell of a sicko...

If he cut the bubbles with his knife, they would just split in two. If he shot them, all it would pop were the bubbles in its direct path.

There was no way for him to break through the wall.

The footsteps creeping up behind him echoed ominously. He had nowhere to run.

White Spider's voice trembled. "How did you know where to find me?"

The answer he got was curt. "I just did."

However, it also echoed with confidence. Bonfire might have actually been telling the truth. After all, how other than sheer intuition could he possibly have known about White Spider's attack?

White Spider turned to the heavens and screamed.

"Why do I have to fight this goddamn monster?!"

The second battle—Imperial interloper White Spider versus Lamplight's boss Klaus—had begun.

Erna seemed to notice the change. Her nose twitched.

"The danger is...gone?"

"That's what I like to hear. Come on, let's go." Monika dashed out of the warehouse.

The girls positioned themselves around Matilda to protect her as they advanced. By the look of it, they had gotten out before the soldiers surrounded them. They wove their way through the rows of warehouses to avoid detection, stopping and changing course whenever soldiers passed in front of them. When they were trapped on both sides, they hid behind the nearest building and waited for the danger to pass.

Their destination was the cargo ship docking area, and it was all thanks to two things that the five of them were able to sneak their way toward it under the cover of darkness.

"Hold it. There's someone around that corner," said Monika, who was using her mirrors to broaden her field of view…

"I'm getting a bad feeling off of the west side."

…and Erna, whose powers of intuition allowed her to sense misfortune.

Matilda stared at the two of them in awe as they wove their way between the soldiers' searchlights as though by magic. Even for an Imperial spy, techniques like that weren't something you saw every day.

Beside her, Thea was just as astonished.

The biggest surprise was Monika.

She retrieved her mirrors as they pressed on, then threw the glass into the ground in front of them, using the reflection to see everything both ahead and behind.

"All right, this way's clear."

Sometimes, she would even use multiple mirrors in conjunction to observe locations too far for a single mirror to spot. If her eyesight wasn't up to the task, she would supplement it with her telescope. Getting its lens in focus while running at full speed shouldn't have been possible, but she made it look trivial.

They were making good time—good enough that Matilda was even starting to run out of breath.

"So answer me this." Thea knew it was a bad time to broach the subject, but she did so anyway. "Why is it that I never see you using that trick during our training?"

"Because I don't."

"So what, you've been holding out on us?"

"You make me sound like an asshole. Using it wouldn't have been enough to beat Klaus, so I didn't. That's all there is to it."

Monika didn't sound the least bit ashamed, but that was just par for the course.

Then Monika stopped in her tracks. "This is as far as it gets us, though."

The place the girls came to a halt at was most of the way to the docking area. They hid behind a truck that was stopped right beside the port.

The docking area was swarming with soldiers. When they strained their ears, the girls could hear them angrily shouting and rushing about all gung-ho in their desire to catch the spy.

Monika calmly analyzed the situation. "Looks like the dockworkers are done evacuating. Now all we need to do is get rid of those pesky soldiers so we can get Matilda into that shipping container."

However, there were a good thirty soldiers stationed around the containers, and their searchlights had the entire area lit up. There wasn't so much as a shred of darkness to be seen. There was no way they were going to be able to break through.

Their opponents were onto them.

"This is bad… It feels like we're surrounded," Erna murmured anxiously.

Thea nodded. "We should pull back for now. We might have to get creative."

They might still get an opportunity to draw the soldiers away. Thea set up another one of the smoke emitters under the truck.

Then she turned to Matilda. "Can you still run?"

Matilda's shoulders heaved up and down, but she managed to pant out an "I—I think so…" Getting there had clearly taken a toll on her stamina.

"I'll carry your things for you, yo!" Annette piped up. She snatched Matilda's toolbox away. Matilda gave her a happy little bow. "Thank you."

After watching that fresh affirmation of their familial bond, Thea turned to their telescope-wielding guide.

"Monika, when we fall back, where should we—?"

"………"

Upon seeing the uncharacteristically grave look on Monika's face, Thea trailed off.

Monika continued peering at her mirrors.

"Hey, Thea," she said, still holding up her telescope. "How're you planning on thinning out the soldiers?"

"It's obvious, no? We'll get close, set up smokers, pull back, and repeat as necessary."

"Dunno how much I like those odds. The first smoker barely even fazed them. They've been trained well."

Thea bit her lip at Monika's rational assessment.

Captain Barth's leadership was probably to blame for the soldiers' clean coordination.

Far more of them had stayed in position than the girls had bargained for. This was threatening to become a rather protracted affair.

"They have, but if we want to minimize risk, this is the only way we can—"

"There you go being soft again." An arrogant grin spread across Monika's face. "Making sure no one gets hurt, making sure no one's in danger… That's a good little girl's strategy."

"What other option are you suggesting we have?"

"A fantastic one." Monika stowed away her telescope and replaced it with her go-to revolver. "Annette, I need whatever explosives and smoke bombs you've got handy."

Annette handed over the weapons before Thea had a chance to stop her.

Monika threw the bomb, then shot it in midair to give it even more velocity. It went flying toward the soldiers.

A moment later, a blast of noise and fire split the night.

"_____!"

"Take Matilda and go."

As Thea stared in blank shock, the two smaller members of the group jumped into action. Erna and Annette each grabbed one of Matilda's arms and started dragging her off at a run.

Monika threw a smoke bomb to cover their retreat.

Thea had yet to move. The soldiers had heard the explosion and were running their way. She wasn't about to leave a teammate behind.

"Do you have a death wish or something?" she asked.

"As if."

Then Monika did something that defied all explanation.

She pulled her mask up and her hood down to cover her face…then leaped out from behind the truck and revealed herself to the rifle-wielding soldiers. It almost looked like she was grinning.

"There she is!"

The soldiers reacted immediately when they saw her. They must have been authorized to shoot the spy on sight. They leveled their rifles straight at her, and five of them got ready to shoot all at once.

The searchlights focused in on her like they would an actress atop a stage.

Monika casually drew her knife and held it in a backhand grip.

"Hey, remember how Klaus deflected Corpse's bullets with a knife?" Monika said, not looking back Thea's way.

The situation couldn't have been tenser. What was she going on about?

Sure, Thea knew what she was talking about. She had seen Klaus effortlessly flick Corpse's bullets aside with her own two eyes. It was a skill that only the most elite of spies could master.

Monika's voice rang with composure. "Let's see if I can pull that off, too."

"Wh—?"

Thea shuddered when she finally understood what Monika was planning on doing. This was ridiculous.

Monika was going to try out a technique she'd never so much as practiced.

And against soldiers! A bunch of them, all at once! Using live ammo!

It was an act of sheer madness.

Monika let out a long exhale and fixed her gaze on the soldiers.

Thea could hear her mumbling under her breath.

"Angle... Distance... Speed... Timing... No focal points or rebounds to worry about, so that's one thing I've got going for me..."

Monika was running calculations. She seriously planned on breaking through the bullets with nothing but the power of math on her side.

Thea needed to stop her. However, Monika was concentrating so hard Thea doubted she'd even be able to hear her.

One of the soldiers barked out an order.

"Shoot the spy! Don't let her get away!"

The sonorous voice probably belonged to the fabled Captain Barth. Gunpowder flashed as the five frontmost soldiers all fired at once.

A satisfying *ting* rang out.

"＿＿＿＿＿!!"

Monika was standing there coolly. There wasn't a scratch on her.

She had dodged four of the bullets and swatted away the fifth.

Thea gawked at her in disbelief, and she wasn't the only one. The shooters were frozen in as much shock as she was.

In fact, even Captain Barth was too stunned to give the order to fire again.

"Huh." Meanwhile, Monika's expression was warm with pride. "Well, that was easier than I expected."

She shot Thea a look as she inspected the side of her knife.

"I'll be the decoy. You take care of the kids."

"……!"

Thea ran.

She was done hesitating. She dashed through the smoke screen and followed after Erna and the others.

Behind her, she heard Monika's voice.

"Let's dance, Captain Barth. Don't worry, I'm not after your life."

She fired a shot, and Thea heard the searchlight shatter. The area descended into darkness.

Then Monika ran in the opposite direction Thea had.

The sound of gunfire started and didn't stop, but it gradually grew more and more distant. Monika was drawing the soldiers away.

All Thea could do was praise Monika and her boundless well of talent.

It's amazing how much easier things are now that she's back on our side!

Thanks to Monika's efforts, Captain Barth's command began falling apart.

The port descended into chaos.

Over at a hotel construction site a little ways off from the port, a pathetic scream split the air.

"Eeeeeeeeeek!"

The teary-eyed man fled as fast as his legs would carry him. The term *single-minded* seemed apropos to describe it. He was running the way a child might, with his mouth open wide and his arms flailing about behind him. He ran this way and that—and every which way, dodging each of Klaus's bullets by the narrowest of margins.

Klaus reloaded. "You know, most spies have enough dignity not to scream like that."

"Shaddap, you! How am I supposed to fight a monster like you, huh?!"

The space had nothing but flooring and support pillars, so that was what the man raced around, deftly avoiding the construction tools scattered about.

Klaus gave chase. Something about this didn't quite fit.

He had a pretty good idea of why Thea and the others hadn't called in—they were trying to help someone related to Annette escape. Whether they were making the right choice or not, Klaus knew that the main thing he needed to worry about was that spy's allies.

Just as Inferno would swoop in to save their compatriots when they bungled a job, the Empire was likely to send in skilled reinforcements.

Knowing that, Klaus had sniffed out a man who practically radiated sketchiness.

He had followed him somewhere with no bystanders and attacked him, but there was just one problem—the man seemed far too weak.

Who exactly is he?

His inability to get a read on the man left Klaus befuddled.

"God DAMN, you're fast! Gimme a breeeeak!"

The man continued wailing as he tried to put more distance between them.

Between his beanie and his mask, it was hard to get a read on his face. He was probably somewhere in his twenties, but Klaus couldn't even be sure of that much.

He's got some legs on him, though, that's for sure...

Klaus was using about 70 percent of his full strength, but it wasn't because he was taking the man lightly. There were two reasons: First, he was keeping an eye out for traps, and second, 70 percent of his strength was more than enough to quash most foes.

Yet the man kept outpacing him.

Even if Klaus tried shooting him, the man would just dodge each bullet by the skin of his teeth without breaking his stride.

And I'm chasing him pretty fast, too. He clearly has some skills.

However, Lily's poison foam was still blocking the exit. His foe wasn't going anywhere.

The man could always try jumping, but Klaus wouldn't mind that one bit. The wounds he would suffer would just make it that much easier to finish him off.

"Wait, this is just gonna come down to a test of endurance!" Klaus's opponent realized the disadvantage he was at, too. He clicked his tongue. "And there's no way I'm winning one of *those* against you!"

In the end, he chose to ascend.

The high-rise hotel was being built from the bottom up, and floors one through seven were past the need for temporary construction scaffolding. However, the scaffolds between the seventh and eighth floors were still in place, and the man used them to flee to the floor above with his sniper rifle in tow.

Klaus immediately gave chase.

The eighth floor wasn't just wall-less—it didn't even have a proper floor yet. All there was to stand on was a lattice of exposed steel girders. If he slipped, he would end up tumbling back down to floor seven.

As the man raced nimbly over the girders, Klaus took another shot at him.

His foe let out a little yelp and tottered as he swatted the bullet away with his knife.

Not many spies can pull off that trick...

The skills the man was using spoke of a spy far stronger than his demeanor would have suggested.

Who in the world was he?

Klaus had no idea. He must be a spy who the Foreign Intelligence Office didn't have intel on yet.

"You seem like you can handle yourself in a fight." Klaus came to a stop atop the girders as he spoke. "Why not try attacking me? Who knows, you might even win."

"C'mon, don't try to bait me." The man stopped as well. "We both know that'd end with me six feet under." He shook his head in exasperation, then squatted in place. "See, me, I'm an intellectual. I sneak in, I sneak out. But fisticuffs? I'm not about that noise."

"I don't know, looks like you have some moves."

"Bite me. It's why I keep getting forced into these odd jobs."

Klaus heard another click of the tongue.

He could only see about half of the man's face, but he could tell how displeased his expression was.

He seems perfectly happy getting chatty. This guy just keeps getting weirder and weirder.

Klaus's uneasiness grew.

He couldn't tell if his foe was supremely confident or scared out of his mind.

"Well, hey, if we're trying to get information out of each other, then I got one for you." This time, it was the man's turn to ask a question. "We haven't heard from our man Deepwater in a while. Did you guys catch him or something?"

"Who?"

"Skinny guy, looks like a corpse, classic romantic, buckets of hubris?"

That definitely rang a bell.

It was Corpse, no doubt about it. Deepwater must have been his Imperial code name, although Klaus didn't know about describing the man as a "romantic."

Klaus feigned surprise. "Never heard of the guy, but if someone with your skills is asking, then I'll have to watch out for him."

"Playing coy, huh? It's okay, you just told me everything I needed to know."

That was a lie, no doubt. Klaus was a good enough liar not to be discovered that easily.

If their conversation went on, all they would end up doing was talking in circles. This was going nowhere fast.

"If I want to find out who you are, I guess I'll just need to catch you first." Once they ended up head-to-head, the time for lies and tricks would be over. Soon, their fists would do the talking. "Perhaps it's time I started taking this seriously." Klaus stowed his gun and drew his knife.

"Gimme a break, maaan…"

The man could wail all he liked, but it wasn't going to make Klaus take it easy on him.

Klaus kicked off hard against the steel girder, but it wasn't to run across it—it was to *slide*.

Due to how humid it was, the damp beams were nearly devoid of friction. Klaus was able to reach the man far quicker than running would have gotten him there.

The man tried to get away again, but this time, Klaus was faster. He kicked off against his girder once more to accelerate and thrust a knife right at the enemy's throat.

The man brought up his arm and just barely managed to block the blow. He must have had something to protect him under his clothes, as the harsh sound of metal on metal rang out. However, blocking the strike wasn't enough to blunt the impact.

Klaus used his strength to shove his foe clean off the girder.

The man hung in the air for a moment, and Klaus used that opening to mercilessly gun him down.

His weapon of choice this time was a revolver. Klaus was a master of the quick draw, and he had honed his skills to perfection. It only took him the blink of an eye to swap his knife to his off hand and shoot. A pair of bullets went whizzing toward his opponent.

The man blocked the first shot with his knife, but the second grazed his face, knocking off his mask.

"Dammit, how is this supposed to be fair...?"

He tumbled down to the seventh floor and moaned as he skidded to a stop.

Klaus leaped down after him. This was his chance to overpower and restrain him...but he missed it.

"_____"

Despite himself, Klaus froze.

The man's beanie had fallen off during the fall, and between that and the mask, his full face was now exposed.

Klaus was at a loss for words.

The first thing he noticed was the man's mushroom-shaped hairdo. The man looked youthful, probably in his early twenties, but the hair drowned out everything else and made it hard to focus on the rest of his appearance.

"Even you, huh?" The man tidied up his hair. "You like it? I'm pretty fond of the do, if I do say so myself."

Klaus shook his head. "That's not it."

What he was surprised about was the fact that he recognized the man. His hairstyle had been different back then, but they'd definitely crossed paths before.

"It's because this is the second time we've met."

"Huh?"

"Back at the Endy Laboratory."

The lab in question was a facility in Galgad that conducted top secret research for the Imperial army under the guise of being a pharmaceutical company.

Theirs was an encounter Klaus would never forget.

Up until now, he hadn't been sure it was the same person. After all, their last exchange had taken place from quite a distance apart.

Now, though, Klaus was certain.

"You're the sniper who killed my master, Torchlight."

Guido'd had a decent shot at surviving, but a sniper's bullet had taken that from him.

The only thing that had given Klaus pause was the discrepancy between the image in his mind and the person before him.

This was a man who'd fled screaming like a coward. Could he really be the person Klaus had spent so long searching for?

"Are you with Serpent?"

Serpent was the mysterious group that had massacred Inferno and taken his mentor's life.

Klaus wanted revenge.

"........." The man silently rose to his feet and swept the dirt off his clothes. "You were able to see me from that far away? You really are a monster."

He looked down at the sniper rifle he'd been carefully cradling and combed back his hair.

"Well, this sucks. Feels like my odds of surviving here just keep getting lower and lower."

The man—who would later introduce himself as White Spider—still made no effort to hide his fear, but a grin spread across his face.

After grouping back up with Erna and co, Thea found a warehouse for them to hide in. It was sealed tight, but Annette's blowtorch made short work of its lock.

They no longer had access to Monika's sight, and even though they still had Erna's intuition at their disposal, the chaos across the port made it hard for her to get a read on much of anything. The way she put it, there were so many ill omens all over the place that she couldn't keep track of them.

The soldiers were in a state of extreme disarray.

"Big Sis Monika is really cutting loose," Erna murmured.

There were dozens of soldiers hot on Monika's tail, and she was having to flee for her life amid a rain of gunfire. One wrong step could be her last, and as if that wasn't bad enough, she was operating under the disadvantage of not being allowed to kill any of her pursuers.

They couldn't afford to let the opening she'd given them slip away.

"Once the coast is clear, let's split up and look for that container. Remember, it's blue and says 3-896. Annette, are your radios good to go?"

Thea turned to Annette, who was rummaging around in her skirt.

Annette pulled out four small transceivers, but a moment later, she cocked her head to the side.

"They're bad to go. I think they're broken, yo."

"What?"

Thea was flummoxed. This wasn't where she had been expecting things to go wrong. Then Matilda cut in from beside her.

"Sooo, I suspect the army people are jamming us."

"Can you get around it?"

"Sure, just give me five minutes."

Matilda took the tools from Annette—"May I?"—and began modifying the transceivers, disassembling them with sure, practiced movements and adjusting the wiring inside them. Annette watched her work with obvious glee. "Wow, I'm learning so much!"

Over to the side, Erna let out a subdued murmur. "I........." Thea could sense her unease.

Matilda was an Imperial spy.

By the look of it, she was probably a better operative than they'd given her credit for. When it came to machines, she clearly knew her stuff.

And they were about to help her escape.

"............."

Thea had considered that, too, of course.

A soldier walked into the warehouse. He was beefy in a chubby sort of way.

"""____!"""""

Erna, Annette, and Matilda all went into high alert.

Thea spoke up. "Don't worry; he's with me."

Earlier that afternoon, Thea had successfully won over one of the soldiers by going to him when he was eating lunch all by his lonesome and seducing him. Now he was on their side.

Erna let out a big exhale. "P-please don't scare us like that."

"Sorry about that. I didn't know if we'd even end up meeting him."

That was a lie. Thea had actually gone out of her way to keep the man's existence a secret from the others.

She took the troop deployment intel he gave her, then sent him on his way with instructions to cause a disturbance and a whispered promise to "thank him properly later." At that last part, his whole face flushed red.

Thea shot a covert glance at Matilda, who had already gotten back to modifying the transceivers.

"............"

Thea was going to have to have words with her.

Matilda finished her work in what seemed like no time at all. "Whew. All dooone."

Thea nodded. "All right, let's go."

The girls rushed out of the warehouse and ran toward the docking area at full speed. Luckily for them, there were dozens of shipping containers slated to be loaded onto other freighters lying around, as well as loads of wooden crates and barrels. There was no shortage of spots where they could hide.

There were a few soldiers still stationed around the containers, but the man Thea enthralled fixed that problem for them with a well-placed lie. The soldiers cleared out of the area.

The searchlights that had so thoroughly illuminated the port were all broken. The girls had Monika to thank for that, and due to their honed spy skills, they were able to make their way through the darkness without any problems.

The chaos had served its purpose, and wherever the container they were looking for was, it was undefended.

All they had to do now was split up and find it. Annette and Erna ran off.

"Hey, Matilda?" However, Thea didn't leave Matilda's side. She called out to her after the other two left. "Could I talk to you for a minute?"

"Now's not a great time, Thea. We need to focus on finding that container."

"It'll only take a second." Thea tried to start a conversation, but Matilda didn't bite.

"The longer it takes us to find it, the more danger the others will be in."

If Thea could just look her in the eye for three seconds, she would be able to find out what Matilda desired. But Matilda kept averting her gaze before she could get a chance to.

"This is important." Thea grabbed Matilda's arm. She was tired of waiting. "Tell me—were you about to kill that soldier just now?"

".................."

Matilda went silent—and it was the kind of silence that meant Thea had hit a nerve.

"I saw the murder in your eyes, and I saw the way you held that screwdriver like you were going to stab him in the throat. And from how quickly you moved, it looked like it wouldn't have been the first time."

".............."

That was the reason Thea had kept the soldier a secret from the others—to suss out Matilda's true intentions.

"So what's going on? As I recall, you told us that you had never killed before."

".............."

"I want an answer. If you don't tell me what's going on, then as of right now, you're on your own."

"Oh?"

Matilda shook Thea's hand off in annoyance. It was a strangely rough gesture coming from someone who was normally so meek. Then she covered her mouth with her hands like she was trying to hide her laughter. Thea had never seen her act like that before.

"You didn't juuust start being suspicious of me, did youuu?"

"——!"

The voice slithered through Thea's ears like sludge.

She could hear muffled laughter coming from between Matilda's hands.

"It's too late for thaaat. I mean, how duuumb would you have to be to only start suspecting me nooow?"

"You've been playing us, then?"

"Of course. At first, I was just going to use my daughter as a tool to flee the country with, but you all were so shooockingly useful that I decided to go along with your plan. It was so helpful of you, how you ate up every lie I fed you."

"Why, you—!" Thea thrust her pistol forward.

Matilda was showing a whole new side of herself, and Thea wasn't about to let that stand.

"You're not going anywhere. I'm putting you down!"

She had Matilda's forehead square in her sights.

However, her target didn't seem worried in the slightest. Matilda's drawl took on a provocative tone. "What are you waaaiting for, then?"

Thea placed her finger on the trigger. "I'll do it, you know."

"Oh, go ahead. I do wonder how you'll explain it to my daaaughter, though." Matilda twiddled her fingers with her hands still clamped over her mouth. "Are you really going to tell her that you changed your mind about saving me, so you killed me instead? After you spent all that time building up her hopes? How hooorrible. It's not like you have any proof."

"I don't—"

"You can't do it, can you? You don't have a proper reason to kill me. After all, my acting was perfect."

"......!"

"Thea, honey, you're a nobody. You're too soft, and you're incredibly easy to manipulate. In all my life, I've never met anyone as easy to take advantage of as you." After saying her piece, Matilda smiled. "It's too late. You lost the moment you brought me out here."

Thea bit her lip.

Seeing Matilda's true nature out of the blue like that filled her with a profound rage. That, and the knowledge that she had a duty to shoot her where she stood.

Did Matilda really think she was going to take that sort of provocation lying down?

She needed to eliminate her. But right when Thea started to squeeze her trigger finger—

"Just kidding, of course! ♪"

—Matilda lowered her hands away from her face.

The smile behind them was as gentle as a saint's.

"I really am grateful to you, and I truly do love my daughter. When I get home, I'm done being a spy for good. And about the 'murder' you saw in my eyes earlier, that was just me being surprised. That's the truth, I swear. I've been doing intelligence work for a lot longer than you have, so I just thought I'd tease you a bit. I hope you didn't take any of that seriously, did you?"

"I......"

Matilda softly tilted her head to the side. All the scorn in her voice was gone like it had never been there.

Her smile was truly that of a mischievous older friend playing a harmless trick. The change in her expression was so stark it was like looking at an optical illusion.

"You wouldn't kill me over a joke, would you?"

"............"

"Not when you own friend calls me Mom so lovingly."

"_____!"

Despair crashed over Thea.

Matilda was right. She didn't have a good enough reason to shoot her.

Could she kill Matilda because she might have wanted to murder the soldier? Did Thea have it in her to put someone to death off of intuition alone?

Alternatively, what if she killed Matilda because she wasn't trustworthy? Would Thea be able to justify that decision to Annette?

Matilda was right. She had Thea completely beat.

Whether she knew how Matilda truly felt or not, she still had no choice but to save her.

Thea's finger trembled, then went limp. She couldn't do it. She couldn't pull the trigger.

A voice came in over the transceiver. It was Annette's.

"I found the container, yo!"

Matilda smiled. "Shall we be off, Thea?"

".........Yeah," Thea murmured lifelessly. She lowered her gun.

She didn't have the time she needed to figure out if Matilda was telling her the truth.

Moreover, she didn't have the means to. Every time she tried meeting Matilda's eyes, Matilda simply averted her gaze.

Thea's only option was to go along with her.

The container Annette found was sitting just outside the docking area. It was hard to see it well in the darkness, but it definitely looked blue, and the number 3-896 was featured prominently on its side.

Annette had already unlocked it, and the container's door was wide open. It was loaded full of sacks of flour, but there was definitely enough room for a single woman to fit inside as well.

Matilda walked right on in. "It looks like this is where we part ways. Thank you all so much for everything."

She gave them a radiant smile. Was it a smile of relief or a smile of victory?

"Annette," Thea said through half-gritted teeth. "I'll give you thirty seconds."

"For what?"

"To say your good-byes. Go ahead and make them as heartfelt as you can."

That was Thea's one last feeble act of resistance—appealing to Matilda's feelings for her daughter. The best she could do was try to have Annette use her words to attempt to get her mother to honor the bargain they'd made.

Annette's face was blank. She didn't understand what Thea was getting at.

Matilda, too, just looked at Annette.

"..........................."

"..........................."

The two of them spent the first ten seconds just standing in silence. It was the restaurant all over again.

Right when Thea started quietly panicking, though, Annette finally spoke. "Oh right, I almost forgot." She clapped her hands together. "Here's your toolbox back, yo."

She picked up the toolbox lying by her feet and offered it to Matilda. She had been carrying it in her place while Matilda recovered her stamina.

"........."

Matilda didn't take it. After staring intently at it for a moment, her expression softened.

"——," she said, calling Annette by her original name. "Do you want to come with me?"

"Nope." Annette shot her down. "Being with these guys is fun."

"I see..." Matilda nodded. "In that case, you can keep the toolbox. It'll be my present to you."

"Are you sure?"

Annette's eyes gleamed. Then she hiked up her skirt, rummaged around in it, and pulled out another toolbox.

"Then you can have mine. It'll be like a trade, yo."

Matilda's eyes went wide.

The toolbox Annette had just produced looked exactly like hers.

They were identical, down to their cobalt-blue coloring.

"They're spitting images," Matilda murmured. "You made this?"

Thea thought back.

As part of their plan to defeat the band of thieves, Annette had copied Matilda's toolbox in exacting detail. By the look of it, she had also taken to using it for its intended purpose.

Annette smiled. "Now we match, Mom!"

A noise escaped Matilda's lungs. She took the toolbox with a complicated expression on her face.

"...Good-bye, now."

"Good-bye."

Those were the final words they exchanged.

Annette's smile remained as innocent as could be as she closed up the container.

Thea could do nothing but watch.

"........................"

She hoped that the woman's daughter's words had been enough to move her heart, but—

"Sis," Annette said as she grabbed Thea's hand. "Thank you for hearing me out and granting my wish."

She gave Thea a toothy grin.

Thea squeezed her hand back.

I guess thinking about it isn't going to get me anywhere. She'll keep smiling now, and that's what's really important.

At any rate, they were past the point of no return. Regretting her choices wouldn't actually change anything.

All she could do now was trust in the innocent smile here before her eyes.

The first battle—the chosen members of Lamplight versus Welter Barth and his soldiers—was over.

The soldiers had fallen into disarray, and girls had successfully gotten Matilda past them.

Victory went to Lamplight's chosen squad.

Over at the hotel construction site, another battle was approaching its conclusion as well.

From start to finish, Klaus had been in control.

His foe White Spider had been stripped of his mask, and Klaus had gotten a good look at his face—the face of the man who'd killed his mentor Guido.

A Serpent member, in the flesh...

Klaus gripped his knife.

The coincidence had caught him by surprise, make no mistake, but this was a golden opportunity. Forcing the man to talk could shed a lot of light on why Guido betrayed them and what Serpent really was.

He shifted his center of gravity forward and strode toward his foe.

"C'mon, man! Quit trying so goddamn hard to beat me!" White Spider screamed as he shrank backward.

It really was difficult to imagine someone as pathetic as him being an elite agent.

However, that was probably intentional on his part. It wasn't like with Corpse, who had blindly labeled Klaus as his rival. This man was far cleverer, and Klaus had seen his skills firsthand.

"We both *know* you're stronger; you could at least take it easy on me!" White Spider wiped the sweat off his brow. "Look, I get that you mean business. I get that I can't win. I mean, I'm practically pissing my pants over here."

Somehow, Klaus doubted that White Spider was about to start begging for his life.

He made the call—it was time to subdue him before he did anything obnoxious.

"Stay away from me, fiend." White Spider hoisted up the sniper rifle he'd been carrying throughout their exchange. "Take one more step toward me, and I'll shoot."

He wasn't aiming at Klaus. He was aiming out into the city.

Klaus scoffed. "If you're going to threaten me, at least be realistic. You're not going to hit anyone firing blind like that."

White Spider was holding his rifle in one hand with his arm held all the way out to the side.

The people at the port were a good half mile away. There was no way he could land a shot from that distance without using his scope. Plus, even if he did somehow aim accurately, the recoil from a one-handed shot would prevent the bullet from flying straight anyway.

"I mean, I've never tried it…"

White Spider smirked.

"…but I'm pretty sure I'd hit."

"………"

His voice had a creepily prophetic quality to it.

This was no bluff. He, too, had reached a level where his skills bordered on the superhuman.

"And don't you *dare* call me a coward for this. The way I see it, you're basically a walking, talking ball of OP bullshit." White Spider kept his gun raised as he went on. "I'm not the only guy here who got unlucky tonight. You picked the wrong spot to run into me, man."

"………"

"See, I know about your big weakness—how you refuse to lose even a single one of your countrymen. You wouldn't dare let anything happen to the people Inferno loved and protected, would you?"

"………"

Klaus couldn't move.

His loathsome foe was right before him, he was seething with rage, his opponent's methods were despicable—and yet he couldn't move.

The self-proclaimed World's Strongest had been shackled.

"Sorry, but all your info's been leaked. Your traitor of a mentor told us everything—what you look like, your aspirations, your weaknesses, your skills. He even gave us a photo of you. You're tough—hell, you might really be the World's Strongest—but any spy is beatable if he gets exposed like that."

In terms of information, Klaus's opponent held an insurmountable advantage.

Guido's betrayal meant that the Empire knew everything about him.

As Klaus went silent, White Spider went on in evident amusement. "I planted a bomb in that hotel over there under the sofa in the lobby. It goes off in five minutes."

"You could be bluffing."

"You of all people should be able to tell that I'm not."

White Spider knew about Klaus's talents, and now he was using them against him. There was no way Klaus was going to be able to thwart his plan.

White Spider was a man who always came prepared. Klaus showing up would have been the worst-case scenario for him, so he made sure he had a contingency in place for that eventuality. Thanks to his prep work, he was able to deal with even the most irregular of occurrences.

In contrast, Klaus had had no idea who White Spider was, so he didn't have a single countermeasure in place for him.

This was the power of an information disparity.

"You and me, let's make a deal. I'm not trying to get myself killed tonight."

"...Fair enough. You can go." Klaus found himself forced to accept.

It was the only choice he had. He couldn't shoot White Spider if it meant that a soldier would die for it, and if he didn't get going, he wouldn't have time to disarm the bomb.

"One question, though," he said as he stowed his knife. "Why did my master betray us?"

"If I told you, would you join us, too?"

Klaus shook his head. He wasn't in the mood to bargain.

"I figured," White Spider said quietly. "Then I've got one, too. You're going to be telling your bosses about me, right?"

"I've memorized your face in enough detail to draw a portrait. You won't be setting foot in this nation again."

"So I'm going on the Most Wanted list, huh. Well, what name are you gonna give me?"

"What...name?"

"Y'know, to go with the portrait."

Why did he care about *that*?

Sure, Klaus would probably have to come up with a name for him.

It was like with the assassin who was known by the code name Deepwater in the Empire. The Din Republic had no way of knowing that name, so the Foreign Intelligence Office's Director had chosen to dub him Corpse.

Klaus gave the first answer that came to mind. "Mushroom Man."

"Please, just put White Spider. Let me keep at least some of my pride."

Was that his real code name? He could easily end up changing it, but Klaus committed it to memory nonetheless.

"Then know this, White Spider. Next time we cross paths, I'm ending you."

"Trust me, if I never have to see your mug again, it'd be too soon!" White Spider shouted at the top of his lungs. Even now, he still came across as a petty coward. "Next time, we'll send in someone more suited for the job. After all, we know how to stop you now."

White Spider grinned and parted back his mushroomy hair.

"I mean, either way, you're done. You're not the only one whose info got leaked, you know. We've got the Republic's best and brightest, its promising up-and-comers, everyone. You get it yet? We've got answers for whoever you send at us. Your mentor's betrayal cost your entire nation its future."

White Spider's voice rang with confidence, and his expression was that of a man who'd already won.

However, that in and of itself made Klaus certain of something.

"Well, that's a relief."

"Say *what*?" White Spider exclaimed.

"I didn't know how dangerous Serpent was going to be, but it looks like you're nothing special." Klaus had been overestimating his foes. He realized now what a fool he'd been. "Anyone who gets that excited over a tiny win against me is someone I know I don't have to worry about. Are all the other members of Serpent seriously as weak as you? Try not to let me down too much, now."

He held his chest high.

"I still have seven trump cards up my sleeve."

There were seven someones—or rather, eight someones—that the Empire knew nothing about.

Now Klaus was certain. Those girls were the secret weapon that was going to slay Serpent.

He and White Spider stared at each other.

The man's eyes burned with frustration and confusion, but the confidence in them remained unshaken.

Klaus got the feeling that their next meeting would come sooner rather than later.

And in all likelihood, White Spider realized the same thing.

The second battle—the one that took place at the hotel construction site—was over.

White Spider successfully escaped, but now his opponent knew what he looked like.

Klaus successfully gained more intel on Serpent, but he ended up letting White Spider get away.

Both sides walked away with new information and fresh bruises. The fight was a draw.

Meanwhile, the *third battle that had started in secret* was about to end in the same unseen way it had begun.

Epilogue

Forgetter

White Spider biked his way down the highway.

Fortunately for him, he was able to pass through the army's net before he got added to the wanted list. Klaus had prioritized disarming the bomb over trying to capture him, and White Spider managed to escape death by the skin of his teeth. That just went to show how powerful having more intel could be.

However, things had gone pretty far off plan.

Running into White Spider had come as a surprise to Klaus, but the reverse was just as true.

Dammit all...

White Spider clicked his tongue in irritation.

I mean, he memorized my face and *figured out I'm with Serpent?*

Hearing about Klaus secondhand was one thing, but meeting him in the flesh had been enough to make White Spider tremble.

The man was a bona fide monster.

The spy team Inferno was the stuff of legends, and Klaus had inherited every skill the team had.

In a one-on-one fight, even White Spider's team Serpent only had about three people who could so much as go toe to toe with him. All of them working together would probably be enough to kill him, but White Spider could hardly justify assembling his teammates from across the globe to take out a single backwater nation spy. Actually, now that he thought about it, maybe it *would* be worth it...

There were a million things he needed to consider. However—

"But hey, I should count myself lucky I escaped from that monster in one piece."

—for now, he was going to take a well-earned breather.

As he turned his thoughts away from Klaus, another topic of note came to mind.

I wonder how our favorite abusive mom is doing?

The whole reason he had even stopped by was because she had gotten herself into trouble. After calling for help herself, though, she had shooed him away just as readily. What a selfish woman.

Also, why were Bonfire's underlings helping her escape?

White Spider couldn't think of a single reason why they would want to do that.

Mysteries upon mysteries.

"I mean, it's not like the kid and I are actually related or anything."

Her words echoed in his ears.

"She was just some baby I found stuffed in the trash at a train station. I figured she'd be a useful prop for my spy work, so I adopted her. I never loved her. Never. I do feel a little bad about how her eye got crushed during the plastic surgery to let her pass as my daughter, though."

"And that's why you abused her?"

"Hmm? Nooo, no. I had a different reason for that."

"What's that?"

"Because she creeped me out, that's why. I could never tell what was going on in that messed-up head of hers. I should've just left her in that trash can. I'm telling you, that kid was twisted to her core."

Matilda spoke matter-of-factly.

"You wouldn't get it unless you met her yourself and felt the way she makes your skin crawl. And when she started growing up, she got even more alien. Eventually, I got so scared of her I just started hitting her over and over. Lucky for me, I ended up beating all the memories out of her, so I was able to ditch her. But now I realize I didn't go far enough. When you're dealing with something defective, you have to make sure you dispose of it properly."

White Spider shared the sentiment. Matilda needed to work out a plan to make sure she hadn't leaked any important information.

However, he never expected her to come up with something so hopelessly cruel.

"I'll give her my toolbox as a gift to remember me by, and before I do, I'll set a bomb inside it. After I finish playing the part of the good mother through to the very end, my daughter will go up in flames."

White Spider was at a loss for words.

The woman's plan was to pretend to love her daughter so the girl would risk her life to help her, then turn around and kill her after all was said and done.

"Just checking here, but they haven't figured out how you really feel, right?"

Matilda laughed proudly. *"Don't you wooorry. My acting's been impeccable. I have my daughter eating right out of my hand."*

She spoke with conviction.

"She and her friends would never even dream of killing me."

She was wholly confident she'd acted the part.

White Spider sighed as he finished thinking back to their conversation.

As far as being a messed-up sicko goes, she'd feel right at home in Serpent.

She might end up being useful down the road. He intended to wring her for all she was worth.

For starters, there was a good chance she was in possession of some valuable information.

Bonfire had looked worryingly sure of himself when he spoke.

"I still have seven trump cards up my sleeve."

"When we rendezvous, I'll need to make her tell me everything she knows about those kids."

At the moment, they knew basically nothing about Bonfire's mysterious band of washouts. Intel on them would be a godsend.

White Spider recited his mantra to himself under his breath.

Know who to fear. Know who not to.

He knew that his reunion with Bonfire was probably right around the corner.

Deepwater—the assassin feared across Din as Corpse—had been captured.

If he caved under interrogation and talked, then Lamplight would soon come to obstruct White Spider's plan.

◇◇◇

Klaus got to work disarming the bomb.

True to White Spider's word, he had set it in the lobby of one of the city's hotels.

From the look of it, the bomb wasn't particularly powerful. If it had gone off that night, the most it would have done was killed one or two people who happened to be unlucky enough to be in the vicinity. However, it wasn't mercy that had inspired White Spider to set it up that way.

To him, killing the minimum number of people necessary to achieve his ends was simply a matter of efficiency. Compared to Corpse, who had gotten drunk on his own power and gone around slaughtering people indiscriminately, it was clear to see which of the two was wiser.

Klaus had told White Spider not to let him down, but that was mostly just him acting tough.

Klaus snipped through the bomb's wiring.

Beside him, Lily spoke softly. "I only saw him for a minute, but...he really did look like a mushroom, didn't he?"

Klaus had already told her everything that happened.

"So he was a member of Serpent, huh? I never thought I'd meet someone who could get away from *you*, Teach."

"He's given us a lot to think about." Klaus nodded. "For now, though, we should go meet up with the others."

Klaus headed to the port to see Captain Welter Barth.

The army was using one of the warehouses as their command center, and Welter was barking orders to his men through the vast array of transceivers laid out before him. There were traces of exhaustion in his face, but he wore the expression of a man satisfied with his work.

Welter was the first to speak. "There's nothing for you to do here. We already took down the enemy."

"Oh?"

"She was a tough one; I'll give her that. If you'd stuck your nose in, you might well have ended up dead."

The other soldiers looked at Klaus with triumphant grins.

He shrugged, making sure to put on a good show of disappointment. "Well, that's a shame. Where's the corpse?"

"We chased her into the sea and shot her dead." Welter scoffed. "Your advice was useless, by the way. Trapping her in the water was so much more efficient. We're still looking for the body, but we'll dredge it up soon enough. You want to wait around for it?"

"I'll pass. It might have washed out too far from shore to find. You did good work, Welter."

Klaus gave him a round of applause.

That seemed to tickle Welter's fancy. He puffed out his chest and crossed his arms as he crowed about his victory.

Klaus went in for a question before Welter's mood had a chance to sour. "By the way, what did the spy you killed look like? Was it same person from the passport?"

"I don't know. She had a mask on, so we didn't get a good look at her face." Welter hesitated for a moment before going on. "One of our guys caught a glimpse of her hair, though. Said it was blue."

Klaus nodded. That was exactly the answer he'd been expecting.

He took Lily, and the two of them left the port and its hustling throngs of soldiers behind and headed for the city's outskirts. There were no warehouses or hotels there, just a couple taverns intermittently scattered around.

Klaus stopped in front of a manhole.

The entertainment district was full of elaborate fountains, meaning its water infrastructure had to be diligently maintained. And that didn't just go for the water supply pipes—it applied to its sewers, as well. The sewer system was laid out beneath the city like a web, and it connected all the way to the sea.

Welter had gone against Klaus's counsel *just the way Klaus wanted him to* and chased the spy into the water.

Klaus lifted the manhole cover.

"Oh, hey, Klaus." Beneath it, Monika was already halfway up the ladder. "Haven't seen you in a while."

She was soaked from head to toe in saltwater, and she gave him a small wave.

"Monika, what are you doing down there?" Lily asked.

"Going for a stroll," Monika replied casually.

Lily was quite sure she had never heard of someone going for a stroll in a sewer while totally drenched.

Klaus, however, simply praised her.

"Magnificent."

It began to rain.

Thick black clouds had been hanging overhead for some time, but they had finally reached their limit. Cold raindrops started pouring down from them. The soldiers were probably going to give up the search for their nonexistent corpse soon and report to their superiors that the Imperial spy was dead.

Monika informed Klaus that she was going to continue her stroll, then started walking away. She wanted to retrieve her tools before the soldiers found them, no doubt.

"Oh, right," she said, having remembered something right as she was about to leave.

"Hmm?"

Monika gave him a light shrug. "I wish you'd told me ahead of time that we had someone like *her* on our team. Coulda saved me a whole bunch of worrying. I ended up looking like a fool."

And on that one-sided note, she left.

She was a sharp one, that Monika. By the sound of it, she had already picked up on some of what had happened.

Klaus and Lily headed to the hotel Monika had told them about. It was a dirt-cheap establishment sandwiched between a series of miscellaneous brothels and eateries.

Klaus knocked on the door, and Thea replied anxiously from inside.

"Monika, you're back?"

The door soon opened. Thea was behind it with a look of delight on her face, but her eyes quickly went wide.

"T-T-Teach?!"

"YOUUUUU LITTLE...!" Lily charged into the room, weaving her way around Thea as the latter stood shell-shocked in the doorway. She charged as fast as she could toward the girl sitting on the bed. "Ernaaa!"

"Huh?" Erna's eyes went wide, too, at Lily's sudden onrush.

"You didn't even call! You can't *do* that! Think of how worried I was!"

For some reason, Erna was the sole target of her attack.

Lily hugged her tight, then began relentlessly rubbing her cheeks. Erna yelped and tried to resist, but Lily started tugging on her cheeks undeterred.

Thea looked down awkwardly. "I, um, Teach, we had a good reason we couldn't call ahead; we just—"

"Thea." Klaus cut her off. "If you're doing something you believe in, make sure you see it through to the end."

"Wh—?"

"You're all fine, and that's what matters. Your eyes are a little sharper than before."

Thea's face contorted, and her eyes welled up. She stumbled over her words for a moment. She only just barely managed to keep from breaking into tears.

After subtly wiping the corners of her eyes, she stuck her tongue out.

"Sorry, Teach. We were having so much fun that we forgot which day we were supposed to come back."

"I see. Next time, make sure you report in."

The truth was that he had one or two things he wanted to tell the girls off about.

There was no mistaking that they'd gotten themselves into a dangerous situation, and if they'd consulted with him, he could have led them down a different path and helped them resolve the situation without having to put themselves at so much risk.

However, the four of them had finally come together and overcome hardship as a team. Klaus couldn't have asked for a better outcome.

He decided to just turn a blind eye to what they'd done.

Over on the bed, Lily was still squeezing Erna's cheeks.

"Take that! You were 'having too much fun,' huh, Erna?!"

"Stoooooop!"

Erna's scream echoed through the room. It still wasn't clear why she was the sole target of Lily's assault.

Then Klaus realized something. "Where's Annette?"

The ash-pink-haired girl was nowhere to be seen.

Thea frowned awkwardly. "She... She said she wanted to be alone, so I didn't ask."

Klaus nodded in understanding. He had a pretty good idea of where she was.

She was off watching the battle's conclusion.

Klaus was well aware of why Monika had been worried.

Ruthlessness is something that Lamplight's members are sorely lacking.

It was a legitimate concern. In fact, it was so legitimate that Klaus had considered the exact same thing. When he was first putting the roster together, he had noticed the one trait that none of them had.

Lenience could never exist on its own in the world of espionage.

We need someone who can become as ruthless as they need to be when the chips are down.

Klaus had made countless visits to the spy academies looking for someone who fit that description.

Running across *her* could have been an unbelievable stroke of good fortune.

"I promise you, you don't want her on your team," the principal at her academy warned Klaus when he first came around asking about her. "She's so impossible to control that we're planning on failing her."

Her code name was Forgetter.

At first, it seemed like a simple enough reference to her amnesia, but apparently, that wasn't it.

There was a turn of phrase—"to forget oneself."

It was a saying known all across the world. There were a number of subtle variations—to lose oneself, to forget one's place—but by and large, it was universally understood to mean flying into a rage or becoming utterly obsessed with something.

In short, it was when someone was so fixated on one thing that they lost sight of everything else—they *forgot* themselves in it.

It was really kind of an odd expression. After all, when someone "forgot themselves," what they were actually forgetting was everything else.

To them, nothing mattered besides that single impetus welling up within them.

All that remained was their own desire. It was the ultimate act of pure egotism.

Klaus decided to recruit the girl.

The rain gradually picked up in intensity, rapping ever harder against Klaus's umbrella.

Annette was standing on top of a cliff with a fantastic view.

As a matter of fact, it was pretty close to the hotel where Klaus and White Spider had fought. From there, you could see the entire port.

Rain poured down on Annette as she peered through her binoculars. When Klaus approached her, she swiveled his way, binoculars and all. "Bro!" she exclaimed. "I'd better flee." She turned around and made to dash off.

"Caught you." Klaus grabbed her by the shoulder. "The game of tag is over now, Annette."

For some reason, she laughed in delight. "Finally, yo!"

It was like watching a child at play.

Klaus shifted his umbrella over so it was covering her as well as he gazed down at the port.

The soldiers had given up looking for the corpse, and they withdrew from the area, confident that they had shot the enemy spy dead. Meanwhile, the dockworkers were starting to load in the containers from the docking area. They were working quickly so as to make up the lost time from the earlier commotion.

At the moment, they were using a crane to lift one of the containers into the air.

"Are you watching the container?" he asked.

"Yup. I'm watchin' it like a hawk, yo."

Annette kept her gaze fixed through her binoculars like a schoolgirl on a bird-watching trip. Amid the sound of rain falling, Klaus could hear her humming. It sounded like an original composition.

He raised his own binoculars and looked at the shipping container currently being lifted. It had an ID number printed on its side—3-696. When he compared that number against the port's manifest, everything became clear.

"When I was putting Lamplight together, you were the person who gave me the most pause."

Annette peeled her face away from her binoculars. "Hmm. Did you not want me?"

Klaus shook his head. That wasn't it. "I was worried about you. I knew you might end up having to take on a difficult role all on your own."

"Wait, I've been taking on a difficult role?"

".........."

Apparently, she hadn't even realized it. Klaus wasn't sure if that was something to be happy about.

"I can guess what happened," he said. "There's a woman in that container. What's her name?"

"Matilda."

Annette answered all his questions without hiding a thing.

She told him about how they met Matilda, the dinner at the restaurant, the way they bailed her out, how they found out she was a spy, the fight between Monika and Thea, and finally, how they helped her flee the country.

The way she talked about it, it was like she was recalling a series of fond memories.

"And?" Klaus asked. "Did you enjoy your vacation?"

"It was super fulfilling, yo." Annette did a little hop. "I learned a lot. At first, I didn't understand why the others were making such a big deal about moms. It didn't make any sense to me. It didn't make sense at the pool, it didn't make sense at the restaurant... I didn't get it, yo."

"I see. And do you feel like you understand moms better now?"

"Yup! I've become one step wiser." She smiled, flashing him her pearly whites. "Mom is someone who gets mad at me sometimes, praises me sometimes, teaches me all sorts of things, and supports me in what I want to do. So when I see her all sad, it makes me real angry. That's what a mom is!"

Klaus was surprised.

Annette's voice rang with understanding and conviction. It was a notable departure from the impression he had of her. The Annette he knew wouldn't have come up with anything nearly so concrete. She had changed a bit over the last few days.

However, there was one thing he needed to make sure of.

"And this mom of yours," he said, watching her inquisitively. "Is it Matilda?"

"Nope," she replied. "It's Thea. That woman isn't *fit* to be my mom."

It was a cold, dismissive way of putting it.

Annette's eyes were deep and dark.

Klaus felt a faint tingle run through his fingertips. There was a malice in the air more intense than even the most elite of spies could give off. It was hard to even believe it was coming from the cherubic youth standing beside him.

"As I thought. You figured out what Matilda was really like, didn't you?"

Matilda was the one who had butchered those five thieves. Thea and the others didn't seem to realize it, but she was a dangerous foe who was willing to kill like it was nothing.

"When did you figure it out?"

"The day after we found out she was a spy. She smelled bloody when she showed up by the coast, and there were police running all over the place."

"Makes sense."

"I was furious at her, yo." Annette puffed up her cheeks. It was adorable. "She shows up out of nowhere, and when we're nice enough to get her tools back for her, she goes and kills people. It's like, after all Sis did for her, this is how she decides to act?"

"But you didn't turn her over to the army, did you?"

That would have been the easiest solution, and Monika had very nearly gone and done just that.

Annette shook her head. "An Imperial spy used the tools we got back for her to kill our citizens."

"………"

"If those army punks found out, it would've been a huge scandal for Lamplight, right?"

Bingo.

On top of that, Matilda was Annette's mother. That meant that a girl who worked for their own intelligence agency was not only the daughter of an enemy spy, but she'd even helped her retrieve her tools, and people had lost their lives as a direct result.

The victims may have all been criminals, but if someone with malicious motives got ahold of that information, they could use it to bring the Foreign Intelligence Office under fire. It was the exact kind of scandal the army was just dying to dig up.

"That put you in awkward spot," Klaus said, summing it all up. "If the army managed to catch Matilda, they would get dirt on you. Your time limit was fast approaching, but I wasn't there to get the situation under control. And most importantly, you were livid."

Those factors had led her to one conclusion.

"That's why you decided to assassinate her."

"You got it! You're good at this, Bro!" Annette gave him a round of applause.

That was the third battle—the war of deception between Matilda, the woman pretending to be a loving mother, and Annette, the girl pretending to be an innocent daughter.

By now, it was clear who the victor was.

"So by pretending to help her escape, you were able to trap her in that shipping container."

Klaus took another look at the number on the container's side.

The box Matilda was sealed in was unique and poorly suited for escaping in.

Had nobody noticed?

No, that wasn't it. Thea would have made sure to double-check the container number.

"Ah, you swapped them by using a paint that dissolves in water to draw over the ID number and get her into a different container than planned. Then the rain washed away the paint and revealed the original number."

"Wow! Right again!" Annette clapped once more.

That much was easy enough to deduce. Nobody with good intentions would put a fugitive into that particular metal box. Shipping containers were tightly sealed spaces with no air conditioning or toilet. A single day in one of those would be enough to drive the average person mad.

There was a ship in the port making the fifteen-hour journey to Lylat, and that was probably the one Annette's target thought she was getting on.

The thing was, Annette had put her on a different ship entirely.

"That container's being loaded onto a freighter headed across the ocean," Klaus noted. "Just for the record, is there any danger of her escaping?"

"Nope! The tool I gave her to escape with was totally broken, yo."

Shipping containers were made for the exclusive purpose of shipping goods in bulk quantities. The prospect of someone being trapped inside one had never come into the equation, and they were designed to never open from the inside, no matter how rough the journey got for the goods inside.

In short…

"So Matilda will spend up to ten days locked in there—long enough for her to starve to death."

By the time the container reached its destination, it would become home to a malnourished corpse covered in its own excreta.

Annette flashed him a cherubic smile. "That's what she gets for making me mad, yo."

It was cold-blooded, but there was no denying how effective of an assassination method it was. The army and Annette's teammates would end up none the wiser.

All that was only possible because Matilda had gotten careless, lured into a false sense of security by the fact that the rest of Lamplight had been honestly trying to help her escape. She hadn't even put up a fight.

"Are you sure you went far enough, though?" Klaus commented. "Once Matilda figures out what's going on, there's a chance she calls for help and gets it. Her metal prison will be thick, but there's still a chance that someone on the boat hears her anyway."

"I'm a kind person, so I decided to show her mercy and leave her that tiny one percent chance of surviving."

But right when Annette finished explaining, lo and behold—

—the shipping container exploded.

Fire gushed forth from it as it hung suspended by the crane, engulfing the container in the blink of an eye and transforming it into a blazing coffin.

"But now even that one percent got blown away!"

The light cast by the intense flames served as a black light, making it impossible to see Annette's expression.

The container had been transporting flour, and its black smoke rose high into the night sky.

The dockworkers hurriedly lowered the container to the ground.

Annette nodded as she looked down at them from on high. "Matilda made the bomb herself. She planted it and set it off all on her own."

Klaus was well aware of Annette's talent. She had the ability to make perfect copies of things, down to their tiniest dings and scratches.

She must have switched something out.

It would have been something she and Matilda both had—a toolbox, maybe. While they were making their way across the port, Annette had noticed the bomb Matilda planted in her toolbox and reverse engineered it.

Matilda's plan was to give Annette her toolbox and use it to blow her up.

However, Annette had turned that plan against her, and Matilda ended up self-destructing.

"Pathetic, blowing herself up like that." Annette sounded almost bored. "If she hadn't tried to kill me, she might have lived."

Annette was right.

All Matilda had to do was abandon her plan to murder her daughter, and this tragedy could have been avoided.

She didn't deserve a bit of sympathy. She didn't, and yet…

"……………"

The sudden conflagration had sent the dockworkers into a tizzy, but fortunately, it didn't look like any of them had gotten hurt. Sooner or later, they would discover the charred corpse inside the container. The container's tight seal meant that its insides had quickly reached ultra-high temperatures, and the body was going to be damaged so badly it would be difficult to identify.

Klaus wondered how Thea would feel if she found out what had happened there.

She would be aghast, no doubt, at how Annette had taken advantage of her goodwill to assassinate her mother.

That was why Annette had kept her plan from her teammates.

She had worn a righteous smile and manipulated those ignorant to her true nature in order to achieve her ends—the way the truly evil did.

"Bro..." Annette looked over at him. "...Are you going to call me sick and twisted?"

The question came abruptly, like it had escaped from the depths of her heart.

"What do you mean? Did someone say that about you?"

"I got... Hmm? Huh, I can't remember."

"...Weren't you the one who brought it up?"

"I get the feeling that someone used to say that to me all the time, though," she said cheerfully. "Whenever I did anything, they'd always say that I was twisted to my core."

"........."

That was no great surprise.

When Welter's military intuition picked up on the malice Annette was exuding as she lurked within the city, he had said more or less the same thing. *"There's a great evil at work here, Bonfire—someone so wicked their soul is twisted to its core."*

Someone from Annette's past must have said that to her, too.

Matilda, perhaps. Either that or one of her academy teachers.

Klaus shook his head.

That's not it. They're all fools who can't see what's right before their eyes.

He rejected that rejection. The fact of the matter was that she had made the right call. Her methods may have been suspect, but they had gotten results.

After all, how would things have played out if Annette hadn't acted when she did?

Matilda's desperation might have driven her to attack the soldiers head-on, and people could have died.

The army might have gotten their hands on a pointless scandal to use against them.

Or Matilda, a woman whose acting skills alone made her a powerful enemy, might have gotten away.

Any of those things might have happened if a single ruthless girl hadn't stepped in and manipulated Lamplight, the army, and even an Imperial spy.

Thanks to her, things ended the best possible way for their nation.

"Annette, that mercilessness of yours is a weapon that nobody else on the team has. How could something like that possibly be twisted?"

If anything was twisted, it was the world itself. And in that twisted world, Annette had made the right call.

"That was magnificent. You make me proud I chose you for the team."

A team comprised solely of the virtuous could collapse under the slightest pressure. The world they lived in wasn't a soft place made of nothing but pillows and marshmallows. Sometimes, you needed to be hard if you wanted to survive.

For a team to be as strong as it could be, it needed to be made up of all sorts. Those differences were what gave it its power.

Sometimes, fighting evil required the use of a greater evil.

Klaus had known that, someday, there would come a time when they needed someone who was pure, unadulterated evil on their side.

That was the role he had cast Annette in—Lamplight's weapon of last resort.

"Love ya, Bro."

Annette leaped at Klaus in joy and wrapped his neck in an embrace.

"Don't jump on me."

Despite his order, Annette didn't so much as loosen her grip.

"I refuse, yo."

She dangled off of his neck, sopping wet from head to toe. The water dripping off her seeped into Klaus's clothes.

"Just for you, I'll let you in on my last secret," she said, still dangling. "You see, there was another reason I killed Matilda."

"And what was that?"

"She insulted me. I killed her, and I'm *still* mad."

She scaled Klaus's chest and whispered in his ear.

"After four years apart, she had the nerve to say that I hadn't changed a bit."

That one sentence was what had inspired Annette to kill her mother. There was no way Matilda could have seen it coming, but she had incited Annette's wrath. No amount of playing the loving mother could have saved her.

Once Annette forgot herself, there was no stopping her runaway bloodlust.

That was why Matilda had failed to win over her daughter.

That was the turning point that had led to Annette doting on Thea and hating Matilda.

The great evil spoke in a voice as pure as an angel's.

"I *know* I'm not getting taller. It sucks, yo."

Next Mission

"............"

Thea stood gloomily out on Heat Haze Palace's veranda.

It had been a full day since they got back from the Annette Incident—which was what they'd taken to calling the situation with Matilda—but she just couldn't seem to cheer up. She put on a happy face around the others, but once she was alone, the only thing she could think of was the mocking way Matilda had looked at her.

Thea had spent the entire last month being tormented by feelings of inferiority.

One after another, she had met and gotten outplayed by spies who were better than her.

First Klaus, then Corpse, then Monika, then Matilda…

No matter how hard she tried, she could never find her way onto the same stage as them.

Being picked for the chosen squad had brought her some pride, but now, even that was gone. Despite Klaus's absence, Grete's team had managed to take down an enemy spy all on their own. What accomplishments did Thea have to her name?

Her idol seemed further away than ever—so far that she wanted to cry.

A voice rose up from behind her. "You seem down."

It was Klaus. He had mugs of freshly brewed tea in both hands, one of which he handed to her.

"Thank you. I'm just a little depressed, that's all."

"Ah. Well, that makes two of us."

"Really? *You* get depressed?"

"You don't have to sound so surprised. I'm human, too, and there are plenty of times when my spirit gets low." He stood beside her. "Even if a mission ends successfully, that doesn't mean there weren't problems. I end up brooding sometimes. 'Were there better options I could have taken?'"

"I never realized..."

Klaus took a sip from his mug. She didn't press him for details, and he didn't offer any. From the sound of it, though, something must have been eating away at him recently.

It was like he had let a hated foe slip away or something.

"................"

Thea was curious about what had happened, but Klaus just drank his tea in silence.

She decided to ask him about something else. "So...what do you do to *stop* brooding, then?"

"I... Well, I'll tell you the boss's answer to that rather than mine."

"Ms. Hearth, you mean?"

"Hers would probably suit you better." Klaus drained his mug. *"Make sure you complete the next mission perfectly—that's all there is to it."*

"That's wonderful. I would have expected nothing less from her."

Thea followed his lead and gulped down the rest of her tea. The liquid, so hot it nearly burned her mouth, washed down her throat and filled her body with warmth. She let out a long exhale.

Klaus nodded. "Let's go. The others should have gathered by now."

Thea followed him to the main hall.

The rest of the girls were already there, all chattering away.

Some of them were self-centeredly trying to leave, but someone else always stepped in to stop them.

"It's too noisy in here; I'm heading back to my room," Monika said with a frown. As she tried to rise from her seat, though, Lily grabbed her arm and refused to let go. "But I wasn't done bragging yet!"

Erna, unable to work her way into any of the conversations, tried to awkwardly slink away as well, but Sara spotted her and gave her a gentle smile. "Miss Erna, how was the entertainment district?" she asked.

"Annette spent the whole time bullying me!" Erna cried.

Annette bounced around restlessly. "Yo, I'm gonna go drink some warm milk," she said and made for the kitchen.

However, Sybilla used her considerable physical abilities to promptly catch her. "Aaand gotcha. Just wait a bit, 'kay?"

"................."

The words got caught in Thea's throat as she watched the lively proceedings.

"What's wrong?" Grete asked.

"No, it's nothing. I was just thinking about how nice it was to have us all back together."

Honestly, she was impressed. It was basically a miracle that a bunch of problem children like them were able to work together the way they did.

Klaus stood before them all and nodded.

"Magnificent."

After opening with his usual compliment, he went on.

"All of you did well on your domestic missions, and you delivered valuable results both for this nation and for this team. Now it's time for Lamplight to move to its next phase."

"What's that?" Sybilla asked.

"After we took Corpse alive, he started talking."

Then Klaus dropped the bombshell.

"We know where Serpent will make their next move. At long last, we have them in our sights."

His audience let out gasps of amazement.

Being able to capture Corpse on what was supposed to be an assassination mission was already bearing fruit. Klaus's hope that someone as skilled as Corpse would have valuable information had been right on the money.

Aside from the fact that they'd wiped out Inferno, almost everything about the spy team Serpent was shrouded in mystery.

What they did know, though, was that Serpent was Klaus's fateful enemy and the reason he'd brought the girls together in the first place.

"So?" Sybilla smiled provocatively. "Who you takin' this time?"

A hush fell over the girls.

The members were all assembled.

Thea, code name Dreamspeaker. A negotiations expert who could intuit people's desires by looking in their eyes for three seconds.

Grete, code name Daughter Dearest. A disguise expert who could freely change her voice and appearance.

Lily, code name Flower Garden. A poisons expert who was immune to poison herself.

Sybilla, code name Pandemonium. A master thief who could hide her presence and steal just about anything.

Monika, code name Glint. A formidable all-rounder, even without her secret area of expertise.

Sara, code name Meadow. A rearing expert who could command a hawk, a dog, and a whole host of other animals.

Annette, code name Forgetter. A tinkering expert who could make a perfect copy of any device and turn it into a weapon.

And Erna, code name Fool. An accidents expert who could sense misfortune in advance and lure her targets into it.

Klaus faced the girls, all of whom had tempered their skills through domestic missions and tireless training, and spoke.

"Everyone. Together, the nine of us are going to find out who Serpent really are."

The girls cheered and pumped their fists.

Klaus gave them the details.

This time around, their mission was to infiltrate a foreign country—a destination that none of the girls had set foot on before.

They were headed overseas to the United States of Mouzaia.

The United States' nonparticipation in the Great War and the fact that they'd supplied goods to the war front had allowed it to rapidly grow and become the greatest powerhouse in the world. Huge swaths of global politics and commerce now revolved around Mouzaia, and the Din Republic was a speck on the map compared to it.

This was going to be their biggest mission yet, a prospect that filled them with nervousness and excitement.

"Thea," Klaus said, "you'll be in charge of all command and control once we get to the mission site."

Thea's eyes went wide. "I what?"

"You're ready for it. You'll have Grete to help you devise plans, but you'll be the one giving orders to the rest of the team."

"W-wait, slow down. Then what will you be doing, Teach?"

Up until then, that had all been Klaus's job.

As their boss, he had been manning the rearguard while the girls went out and did what they did best. That was the way Lamplight had operated.

"Isn't it obvious? You've all grown enough to take some of the load off my back. That frees me up to act in a position I'm better suited for."

He revealed his new role.

"This time, I'll be standing on the front lines."

The girls' hearts quivered with anticipatory joy.

Klaus's intuition bordered on superhuman, and the combat skills he'd inherited from his mentor were second to none.

Now that they were battling their archenemy Serpent, Klaus was going to get to use those abilities to their fullest extent.

Afterword

I know that Volume 3 isn't the greatest place for it, but I hope you don't mind if I take a moment to talk about my writing process for Volume 2.

When Volume 1 got released, there was a character popularity poll on the series' official website. The idea was that whichever of the seven heroines (with the exception of a certain unlucky blond) shone brightest in the poll would get to be on the cover of Volume 2. Volume 2 was going to focus on Grete, so it worked perfectly.

However, there was one thing I was worried about. Right before Volume 1 came out, my editor got in touch with me.

"Takemachi, what if the girl who wins the poll doesn't actually show up in the second book?"

That was an excellent question. My manuscript for Volume 2 was already mostly finished, so if someone like Thea or Monika won, we could have ended up in an awkward situation where the girl on the cover didn't even appear in the story.

It was okay, though. I had a brilliant idea.

"Don't worry!" I replied. "If that happens, I'll just make some quick revisions to the second book's plot!"

As an aside, 80 percent of authors who are about to have their debut work come out are filled with a strange feeling of invincibility (I assume).

I was awash in baseless confidence, and after Volume 1 came out, my editor gave me another call.

"Annette won the poll. Can you go ahead and make those revisions that you said you would?"

"Say what?"

It was incredible. She barely had any screen time in the first book, so I figured she didn't stand a chance, but the combined strength of Tomori Kusunoki's voice acting and Tomari's character design was somehow enough to win her the top spot. Truly, some incredible stuff.

Moved as I was, though, my voiced trembled.

"I'm sorry, but if I try to give her a spotlight, she'll end up destroying the book. She's the one girl I can't fit in."

My editor's internal reaction was probably something along the lines of *The hell did you say?!* I really am sorry about that.

The fact of the matter is that she's the kind of character who gets out of hand the moment I so much as blink. I can have all sorts of wonderful plans drawn up, but with a laugh and a "That's not my problem, yo," she'll go ahead and smash my invincibility to pieces.

In fact, *nobody* can control her—but I guess that's what makes her so likable.

I'd like to take a moment to give another round of thanks to Tomari, who helped make that and everything else possible, as well as the voice actors who helped bring life to the popularity poll. And most of all, I'd like to thank the readers who voted.

Finally, I have some news about the next book. Sorry to keep you waiting, but the wait is over—all the Lamplight members will be working together in this one.

The girls have grown stronger, and it's time for them to face a formidable foe. This is what the whole series to date has been building up to, and I'm going to do my darndest to make sure Volume 4 serves as a fitting finale to the first season of *Spy Classroom*. Until then, that's all from me.

Takemachi